# FAR

# FAR

Book Three of The Freak Series

## Carol Matas

KEY PORTER  BOOKS

**Library and Archives Canada Cataloguing in Publication**

Matas, Carol, 1949-
    The freak III : far / Carol Matas.

(The freak series ; bk. 3)
ISBN 978-1-55470-094-3

I. Title. II. Series: Matas, Carol, 1949- . Freak series ; bk. 3.

PS8576.A7994F37 2008      jC813'.54      C2008-902232-7

 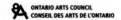

The publisher gratefully acknowledges the support of the Canada Council for the Arts and
the Ontario Arts Council for its publishing program. We acknowledge the support of
the Government of Ontario through the Ontario Media Development Corporation's
Ontario Book Initiative.

We acknowledge the financial support of the Government of Canada through the Book
Publishing Industry Development Program (BPIDP) for our publishing activities.

Key Porter Books Limited
Six Adelaide Street East, Tenth Floor
Toronto, Ontario
Canada M5C 1H6

www.keyporter.com

Text design: Marijke Friesen
Electronic formatting: Alison Carr

Printed and bound in Canada

08 09 10 11 12 5 4 3 2 1

For Lucille Ruth Brask

# ONE

"**D**on't you trust me?"

I can't believe he just said that. I mean, it sounds like a line from a B movie and Jon is *not* the kind of guy to spout B-movie jabber.

I make a quick decision not to demean myself by answering.

"Don't you trust *me?*" I reply. Yeah, that'll show him. Two can play the cliché game.

Silence on the other end of the line.

I wait.

My question, of course, is more loaded than his. When I throw it back at him, he knows what I mean: don't you believe in my *powers?* We're arguing about something I "saw," a flash. This girl, Cindy, is trouble. And since my psychic powers have proven to be right every time, why is he acting like I'm this petty jealous girlfriend? Me, jealous? Hah!

Carol Matas

Okay. Maybe a teeny, tiny bit. But really, that's not what this is about. As soon as Jon mentioned Cindy's name and said she'd been assigned as his new study partner—meaning he was tutoring her in English—I had this flash of blackness. And the last time I had a flash of blackness like that people died. Lots of people, and almost my best friend Susie's mom. So I know there is something bad around this Cindy person. I know it for sure, and I don't want Jon being part of that. Not if he can avoid it. And he can. He simply asks for a different student to tutor. He can do that, I think. Well, he certainly *should*!

Unfortunately, this is all happening long distance, because I'm in Palm Springs with my family for spring break. And Jon, my dreamy almost-perfect boyfriend, is stuck in snowy, minus ten misery while I'm basking in a warm, sunny heaven. Hardly seems fair to give him grief over this girl, but the flash was so strong I couldn't help myself.

I finally take pity on him and break the silence. "Look, I know we trust each other. But this is different, that's all. Something's wrong with her."

"Maybe I can help her then," Jon answers. Typical. In a good way.

"Or maybe you'll just get caught up in whatever it is," I caution him.

8

# Far

"Any idea what that might be?" he asks.

"No," I say, wishing fervently that I had a clue. "I'm not getting anything but this black feeling."

"I'm just meeting her after school twice a week to help her get through *Julius Caesar*." He pauses. "Maybe you're getting the feelings because of the play. You know, betrayal, murder, mayhem—Shakespeare had it all."

"Maybe." I agree not because I believe it but because I'm thousands of miles away and can't do anything about it. I'll be home in a week and hopefully we can talk about it face to face.

School actually started today but we're here for an extra week. My parents figured it made sense after coming all this way and paying tons of money for four plane tickets. We're staying in a condo near Baba in a complex called Cathedral Canyon Country Club. It's a two-bedroom place she rented from a friend when we told her we were coming, right near the one-bedroom she's in. Marty and I have to share a room with twin beds but it's worth it. Annoying younger brothers don't seem half so annoying when you can swim with them every day.

Before we came to Palm Springs, Dad gave a paper in San Diego. That was awesome because we went to Sea World and saw the whales and then walked on the beach and watched people surf, which was so cool. But tomorrow is the big day for me. Tomorrow we're driving to Palm Desert—only about fifteen minutes away—to a university where there's a whole department devoted to psychic studies. And they're going to study me! Yup. And I can't wait because maybe they can help me understand what's happening to me. That's my hope anyway.

Hope. I've been living on it ever since I died and went ... well, somewhere ... and met my Zaida and an angel and was sent back here only to discover that I'm psychic. Really psychic. I get these flashes, but the trouble is they are never exact. They're just feelings that I have to decipher like one of those codes in a James Bond movie. I mean, why, if the universe has decided to confide in me, can't it be more specific? Like, "Jade, you have a bad feeling about Cindy because she's going to accidentally trip Jon as they leave the classroom and he'll fall down the stairs and kill himself." You know, something I can *use,* instead of vague feelings that make your boyfriend think you've lost it.

"Don't trip on any stairs," I say to Jon.

"Did you just see something?" he asks.

"Not really," I say. "It's so frustrating!"

"Maybe you'll get some answers tomorrow."

"We can only hope," I sigh.

"Tell me again about swimming in a pool surrounded by palm trees," Jon says. "I'll live vicariously."

I don't want to ask him what vicariously means. I mean, he's as amazing in English as I am in Math. And that's saying something. I was good before I got these new powers but now I'm in Grade 11 Math instead of Grade 10 with the rest of my class, and I'm ahead of everyone after a couple months. I can just "see" things in my head. Jon is in grade twelve, a problem for Mom and Dad at first, but considering he's the son of Aunt Janeen's fiancé, they've gotten over it.

"Right now I'm sitting on the patio gazing at mountains, palm trees swaying in the breeze and flowers everywhere," I say. I realize that if Jon were describing this view to me it would sound positively, astonishingly gorgeous, whereas all I can do is tell what is. "The flowers are red," I add, at least attempting to help him see it.

"Sounds like heaven," he says.

"Wish you were here," I say.

"Not as much as I do!" He says this with feeling and I don't resent the fact that he probably means because of the weather as much as to see me.

"Please," I add, "just think about changing partners. You haven't started yet so she won't be insulted or anything."

"Uh, yes she will. I can't exactly give a good reason, can I?"

"So she'll be insulted," I say, starting to feel huffy. "So what?"

"So I don't want to hurt someone's feelings," he says. "And even if I do ask, there's no guarantee Mr. Low will listen to me. Why should he?"

"Because it's a voluntary program and you could drop out and they don't want to lose you," I retort with feeling. Why is he being so stubborn? Should I actually be worrying about this girl?

"I'm not a rock star," Jon says, "and I don't want to behave like one."

I get that. Jon's quiet and he doesn't like to make a fuss about things he thinks are petty. And he obviously thinks I'm being petty—or at least pushing him to do something he doesn't want to do.

We seem to be on the edge of our first really big fight.

I decide to back off. Only a week and I'll be home.

"Just be careful," I say.

"I miss you," he answers.

"Me too."

"Call me tomorrow and tell me about the tests."

"I will."

As I hang up the phone I stare around me at the stunning beauty of Palm Springs—the purple mountains in the distance, the riot of colour everywhere—and yet all I feel is darkness.

# TWO

Dad and I are driving out to the university in Palm Desert. It's just the two of us since Mom is going hiking with Marty (who didn't want to be anywhere near a school). I'm pretty nervous. I mean, it's not like I'm taking an exam or anything, but, well, it's kind of close. The people who teach at this university are experts, after all. I found them totally by accident when I was surfing the Web, looking for psychic stuff—you know, to help me understand what was going on with me. And there was this site from the university—an entire division within the psychology department devoted to psychic testing and looking into weird things. They call themselves "The Institute of Anomalous Knowing," or "IOAK." I had to look up "anomalous" in the dictionary. It means "deviating from the norm or from what people expect." Or "strange and difficult to identify or classify." Right. That would be me. Strange and difficult to classify? Like knowing that someone is going to die, for instance, or hearing what people are thinking, or seeing auras, or being able to tell if someone's sick? Yeah, I'd say that's not *normal*!

I sigh.

"What's up, Jade?" Dad asks.

"Nothing. Just thinking about my 'abilities.'"

"Don't knock them," Dad says. "Thanks to you, Susie still has a mom and—well, I don't even like to think what might have happened to those little kids at synagogue that day . . ."

"I know," I say. "I just hope these IOAK people aren't a bunch of weirdos."

"They operate out of one of the top universities in the States," Dad says. "They *couldn't* be a bunch of flakes."

"Like everyone at your university is totally normal, right?" I say.

Dad laughs. "I suppose you have a point. Just because it's a university doesn't mean everyone isn't crazy."

We both know he's joking. Dad loves his colleagues. After all, what could be better than being surrounded by math geeks?

We turn off Highway 111 onto a side street and then into a large parking lot. When we get out of the car the warm air hits me and I can't get over the fact that I'm wearing capris, sandals, and a short-sleeve top instead of a parka. We walk through the gravel lot and then onto a long path, olive trees bowing over us and various cacti planted in the dirt along the sidewalk.

"See how there's no grass, anywhere?" Dad says. "That's the new ecology of the desert. City planners and even homeowners landscape naturally now, using dirt and cacti and native plants so they don't have to waste water keeping the grass green."

I nod absently, getting more nervous by the moment.

Dad glances at the campus map he printed from the website and points us down another path. A large building soars over us, all windows and pale concrete. Students sit outside at tables working on their computers—something you sure don't see at home in the snowdrifts. This must be the place because Dad leads me inside and we climb up a circular staircase to the second floor. We find double doors with the letters "IOAK" on them and walk in.

A secretary smiles up at us from behind her desk. She is a young woman with long dark hair and a necklace made of turquoise stones.

"Hello," Dad says. "I'm Dr. Joseph and this is Jade. We have an appointment with Dr. Black."

Before she can reply a very tall man bustles out of a

door down the hall and races over to us. His thick dark hair is streaked with grey and looks like he has been grabbing it until it practially stands up on end. His eyes are hazel and very large, so along with his wild hair he looks either surprised or like he's stuck his finger in a light socket. He grabs Dad's hand and shakes it so hard Dad winces. Then the man bends over—and since I'm pretty tall, that shows how tall he is—and shakes my hand too.

"You must be Jade!" he says. "So glad you're paying us a visit! And delighted to meet you too, Dr. Joseph," he adds.

"Please call me David," Dad says.

"Only if you call me Nathan," he replies.

"Come with me," he says, leading the way down the hall. "We're all ready for you. You aren't nervous, are you, Jade?"

"Uh, 'fraid so," I say. I know that came out all testy, but he runs a psychic lab, for heaven's sake! He must know I'm nervous!

"Well, there's no need," he assures me as we make our way to the end of the corridor. "We're going to the lab. You'll participate in some simple tests and then we'll have a talk afterwards."

"Oh," I say. "I thought maybe we'd talk first and I could ask you some questions."

"We want you fresh for the tests," he explains, "and even a casual talk might strain the old grey matter. Here we are."

He throws open the door and we enter a large room painted a deep blue. There are small booths, each with two desk areas. The desks are face to face but are separated by a wall. Each booth is enclosed in glass and a few are taken by people doing whatever they do.

Dr. Black points to a booth. Someone is already seated on one side of the wall but his back is to us so we can't see his face. "That's Mitchell—Mitch," Dr. Black says. "He's one of our senders."

"Senders?" Dad asks.

"Yes. He will send Jade images—he'll be holding pictures—and we'll see how many hits Jade gets. It's good that they've never met. We try to keep our studies rigorously scientific. Jade, you'll be wearing earphones connected to me. I'll tell you to write down what you see as Mitch picks up each new card and tries to send you the image. When you get an image, Jade, just speak it aloud. We'll also record everything you say. Ready?"

I glance at Dad. He nods. It all seems pretty straightforward.

"Let's do it," I say.

Dr. Black walks me into the booth and gets me

settled in the chair. I try on the earphones and he moves out of the room. Suddenly I hear, "Testing, testing."

"I can hear you," I reply.

"Then we'll get started," he answers. There is a pause. "All right Jade, Mitch is looking at his first card and is sending the image to you. Just sit quietly, try to empty your mind and say aloud what you see whenever you're ready."

I sit quietly. The booth is soundproof and there is no noise but my own breathing. I close my eyes. And then I do see something—a cabin in the woods, surrounded by pine trees. I say so.

"Next," comes Dr. Black's voice.

I wait. I see wind blowing, waves crashing, and something like a hurricane. I describe it.

"Next."

And so it goes. I see a large mountain. I see the ocean on a sunny day. I see flowers. I see a small room with white walls. I see a large city at night. I see the stars.

Finally Dr. Black says, "That's it!"

I take off the earphones and Dr. Black comes into the booth. He's grinning. "You're pretty amazing!" he says.

"I am?"

"You had an almost perfect score. You saw the pictures almost as if you were looking at them yourself. My dear," he says, taking my hand, "you are the real deal! Come on, I'll buy you and your father a soda."

Dad is waiting on a chair near the door. He gets up and seeing the smiles, he smiles too. Mitch comes out of his booth and Dr. Black introduces us. He's around eighteen—maybe, nineteen—with a round face, carrot red hair, and freckles. He's got a kind of crooked grin and looks like a nice guy.

Dr. Black is effusive in his praise of Mitch, too. "You must have sent her very clear pictures," he says. "She got almost everything. The only real miss, in fact, was when Jade saw a small room with white walls."

Mitch looks startled. "There was no card like that," he says.

"I know," Dr. Black agrees. "But one miss? That's just amazing!"

Mitch says, "Don't freak out. She can't know . . ."

"I can't know what?" I ask him.

Mitch turns pale, and he's pretty pale as it is. "I . . . I didn't say anything . . ."

"Are you okay?" Dr. Black asks him.

"Fine, fine, just tired," he says. "Excuse me, please." He almost runs away, bursting through the lab doors and out into the hall.

Dr. Black grimaces and says, "This work can certainly take a toll." Then he motions for us to move through the doors as well. "Shall we get that drink?"

# THREE

W<small>E FOLLOW DR. BLACK ALONG THE HALL, AND</small> then down the stairs to the main floor. We walk with him across a long foyer and into a wide cafeteria. I realize that I'm starving and when we stand in line I tell Dad I wouldn't mind some lunch. I look at my watch. It's only 10 a.m. I can't believe it! I feel like hours have gone by and that I've run a marathon. Not that I've ever run one, but I have danced for hours and I'm even more famished now than after that.

"Quite normal," Dr. Black says. "Psychic work is very hard. Lunch is on me."

I order grilled cheese, fries, and a sweetened iced tea. We find a table and sit down.

For a moment no one speaks.

"You said you had questions, Jade."

Since I'm busy stuffing a sandwich into my mouth, Dad steps in.

"Tell us how this place got started," he says.

"You mean, how did a Harvard-educated psychiatrist end up in the desert running an institute that most people think is deluded, at best?"

Dad smiles. "Something like that."

"I had this weird experience," he said. "My wife had lost her mother's wedding ring. A colleague dared me to try a dowser—you know, usually you see them with water sticks, but they claim to be able to find anything. So I called this fellow I found online, and without even being there, he told us over the phone exactly where the ring was. Exactly! And that started me thinking. How could that happen? I started reading and asking questions and one thing led to another and it's really a long story, because that was twenty years ago and it took another ten before I accepted that all this was real—'all this' meaning anomalous knowledge— and decided it needed scientific investigation. That's it in a nutshell."

"And you?" he added, looking at me. "You said in your email that you were 'normal' until you had an attack of meningitis?"

"Yes. I almost died and I had a near death experience and met my Zaida and maybe an angel or something, and when I woke up I could hear things and see things and know things."

He gazes at me. "I'd like you to come back tomorrow, Jade, if you could. I'd like to repeat the test with different images but the same sender and see if you can do it again. I mean, those scores are remarkable."

"Good enough for an article?" Dad asks.

"Absolutely!"

They are both kidding—and not. I can tell.

I'm not sure how to react. I mean, part of me was hoping Dr. Black would find I had no ability at all, that it was all a fluke. I never actually imagined such a positive test result and such a big reaction.

I've downed my grilled cheese and now I can ask what I've been wanting to for ages.

"Do you know what this all means?" I say to Dr. Black. "Like, I can see the future sometimes. Does that mean the future is fixed? Or when I see auras or hear thoughts? How can I do that?"

"That's exactly what we're trying to figure out here," he says. "After a number of years of research, we have some theories. We've done some studies that map the brains of psychics while they are 'tuned in' and we've discovered something very interesting. The brains of psychics change while 'tuned in.' But we didn't see more activity in the brain—we saw less."

"You mean we become stupider?"

"No, no, not at all!" Dr. Black laughs at my question,

but it's a nice laugh and it doesn't bother me at all. "It appears, though, that part of the brain actually shuts down while a psychic person is meditating or receiving information about the future or about other people. We think this shutting down allows the person to receive knowledge that otherwise cannot be received."

"So my brain is actually functioning differently, and you can see that?" This is exciting! I've been driving myself crazy ever since I developed these powers, trying to figure out how on earth I could be doing what I'm doing. I've lost count of the times I've asked myself if I'm some kind of freak or if there is a scientific explanation.

"Jade is a brilliant mathematician," Dad boasts. "And, of course, extremely rational. She didn't believe in anything like this before it happened to her— neither did I, for that matter—so it's all been a bit of a shock."

"I'm sure it has," Dr. Black says sympathetically.

"I have to accept that it's real," I tell him, "but I need to figure out why."

"You've come to the right place," Dr. Black assures me. "That's the mission we're on and I believe we're getting somewhere. As well as the changes in the brain, we've discovered another commonality. The psychics we've studied tell us that all beings on the planet are connected and that somehow they simply tap into that connectedness. We are all one, and therefore it's easy to tap into someone else. Somehow, you've dropped your barriers and have learned to get past other people's barriers as well."

This is cool. "So I'm, like, the opposite of closed off?"

"That's right. In a way, you are the person you are reading, and that's why you can read them. You are you and them at the same time."

I am stunned by this idea. It's so simple and yet it makes so much sense. And it's exactly the way I feel when I'm "reading" someone and often can't stop myself. Like I'm them, somehow. It also reminds me of a Beatles song I really like. How does it go? "I am you and you are me and we are one together . . ."—or something like that.

"So, tomorrow? Can you manage it?" Dr. Black asks.

Dad looks at me, maybe worried that I won't want to spend the last week of my spring break inside when I could be at the pool. But this is way better than any sun-worshipping fest.

"If Dad doesn't mind," I say.

"Not at all! It's fascinating to me," Dad says, "and Jade knows I hate sitting by the pool."

"Can't remember the last time I did that," Dr. Black

says. "You take it for granted here and then forget to even bother."

We agree on another meeting tomorrow morning and Dr. Black tells us he's going to see if he can find Mitch.

"He had a kind of weird reaction when you mentioned that thing about the white room, didn't he?" I say.

"I'll ask him about that," Dr. Black says. "So we'll see you tomorrow? And Jade?"

"Yes?"

"I'm glad you found us on the Web. Maybe it wasn't an accident. You might be the best subject we've had here."

With that ringing in my ears Dad and I head out to the car.

We're walking through the parking lot and I'm looking down, trying to make sure I don't get gravel in my sandals, when something very odd happens. I suddenly get a really, really strong feeling that I should duck or sit down or something like that and it's so strong that I grab Dad and pull him to the ground. Just then, something whizzes past our heads and crashes into a car near us, cracking the windshield.

Dad, who is sitting unceremoniously on his bottom, stares at me as I crouch beside him.

"What just happened?" he asks.

"I'm not sure."

He starts to get up but then looks at me first, to make sure it's all right.

"I think it's okay," I say, feeling a little shaky.

"What happened?" he repeats, standing up and brushing bits of gravel off his pants.

"I don't know," I say, pushing myself up. "I had this feeling, almost like a voice was saying, 'get down, get down,' and for a split second I was going to ignore it and then I remembered what Dr. Black said about some people just being tuned in and I thought, 'well, I'd better listen' and I pulled on you and . . ."

Dad inspects the broken windshield. A huge rock is sticking out of it, surrounded by hundreds of little cracks.

"That would have hurt had it hit either of us," he says.

Bit of an understatement. It probably would have killed.

We both look around, but the parking lot is deserted. We're the only ones here and neither of us can see a soul. 'Course anyone could be hiding behind a car.

"Let's get to our car and then I'll call the school and report this," Dad says.

He calls directory assistance once in the car and then informs someone in the university's security force about the incident. He tells them we'll be at Dr. Black's lab in the morning tomorrow should they want to ask us anything, but they say it won't be necessary.

We're both a little creeped out as we drive back to the condo. Was someone aiming for us? Surely not. We don't know anyone here, outside of Dr. Black, Mitchell, and the secretary. . . . So a random attack, then? That doesn't make me feel any better, but I guess it's more likely. Either way, it's weird.

Dad must be thinking the same thoughts as me because he says, "We don't have to go back tomorrow."

"But I'm finally getting some answers, Dad," I say. "I *want* to go back. I *need* to go back."

"You *need* to?" Dad asks.

"I don't know why," I answer, "but I do."

"All right," Dad says. "Then we will."

# FOUR

I SIT ON THE PATIO AND PICK UP THE PHONE TO call Jon. It's great—this condo has unlimited long distance anywhere in North America, so Jon and I can talk as long as we please. Baba is out with her friends playing bridge and Mom and Marty have gone off to the pool. I promised I'd join them as soon as I've called Jon. It's four o'clock here, which makes it six at home, the perfect time to reach him. Plus, I know he'll have just finished his first tutoring session and I can't wait to find out how it went.

He answers on the first ring.

"I knew it would be you," he says.

"Hey! That's my territory," I joke.

"I want to hear all about the big test," he says.

"And I want to hear all about your tutoring," I say, trying to sound just as casual as he does, but maybe not succeeding.

"You first," he says.

"It was wild! Apparently I had one of the best scores ever!"

"Really?" Jon says, and I can hear he is thrilled for me. "Tell me how they tested you, exactly."

"They have a sender, Mitch"—and here I leave out that he's a pretty cute guy—"and he sends out images and I describe what I see."

"And you could actually see the images he was sending?" Jon asks.

"I saw almost all of them."

"Amazing," Jon says.

"And then I got to talk to the director and ask him lots of questions, but I'll need to tell you all that when I get home, and then . . ."

"And then?"

I don't want him to worry so I just mention the rock throwing and try to play it down. That doesn't work, though. He's concerned.

"Do you have a feeling about it?" Jon asks. "Can you see who did it?"

"Not really," I say. "I'm not getting anything at all."

"What's this Mitch guy like?" Jon asks.

"He seems nice," I answer. But I see where he's going. "Dad and I only met three people today and I totally can't see Dr. Black or that secretary trying to

30

hurt me. Why Mitch would either I don't know. Much more likely it was some idiot who wanted to wreck a car or something and didn't see us. Or someone who *did* see us and just wanted to hurt someone, anyone."

"You read about crazy people on campuses all the time, right?" Jon says. "Could be that."

"Probably that," I agree, although I'm not sure how much better that makes me feel.

"So be careful tomorrow," he adds.

"I will. Now you. How was the session?"

"It was good! Cindy's a really talented poet," he declares.

My stomach clenches and I have that bad feeling all over again.

"Is she?"

"Really! I'll text you some of her poems. She can't seem to put her mind to Shakespeare on her own, but when I explain it to her she gets it right away. She's smart, she just doesn't realize it. A few of her poems blew me away."

I still have the bad feeling.

"Jade?"

"I'm here."

"Still have a bad vibe?"

"I do, but that's all I'm getting, still nothing specific."

"Well, so far so good. She's not a drug dealer or

anything. Just a kid who needs help and not even much of that."

"Kid? How old?"

"She's in grade eleven. You can look her up on her wall—Cindy Moss."

Again my stomach clenches. "I don't want to be obnoxious about this or anything," I say, "but if you can trade her for someone else, I still think you should."

There's a pause and I can feel that he's starting to resent my interference. I can also feel he doesn't want to be controlled. Why do I feel, then, that this is exactly what Cindy wants to do to him? I blurt it out.

"She wants to control you."

He laughs.

"How? By mind control? I only see her twice a week. Oh, except I'm going to a poetry slam she's in tomorrow night. Trying to encourage her."

My eyebrows must be up into my hairline. This almost sounds like a night out together. But if I say that he'll think I'm being jealous. I bite my tongue.

"So what else is happening?" I ask. Lame, but changing the subject has got to be better than this.

"The weather is getting better. Snow's starting to melt."

"Well, that's a relief," I say.

We have an awkward silence.

"So, dinner is ready. Talk tomorrow?" he says.

"Sure."

"Good luck with the new test," he adds. "And be careful."

"Thanks. I will."

Baba walks onto the patio just as I hang up.

"Boy trouble?" she asks.

"Why?"

"I can just tell," she says.

Baba is seventy-two and never slows down, not even since Zaida died. She does aerobics, plays bridge, works on political campaigns, and yet she is always there for me.

"I think Jon is getting mixed up with a girl he's tutoring."

"Mixed up?"

"I just have a bad feeling about it—but I'm not sure what it is."

"Your feelings are usually pretty accurate," Baba says.

I nod. "But he thinks I'm jealous. I can tell by the way he's reacting."

"Are you?"

I grin at her. "Moi?"

"You're above all that, correct?"

"Absolutely!" I agree. "But Jon did say I should check her out online."

"That doesn't sound like he has anything to hide," Baba says and she's right. In fact, nothing he's *said* shows he's covering up.

"Well then," says Baba, "let's have a look at her."

We go inside and sit at the dining room table where Dad has left his computer. I log on and then sign in.

"I should join this with my friends," Baba says, checking out the site. "What a terrific way to keep in touch when the winter is over and we all go back to our own homes."

I volunteer to help her get started, but first we have a look at Cindy.

"She's very pretty," Baba says as Cindy's page opens on the screen.

She's got short blond hair, big blue eyes, and a smile that could be in a toothpaste ad. She looks cool and sophisticated, quite the opposite of me with my unruly long red hair, brown eyes big as a doe's and legs so long and lanky I usually tower over everyone—not Jon fortunately. I stare at her. What is it about her that sets me off? Is she evil, manipulative, into drugs, crazy? It has to be something! And it's something that's going to hurt Jon. Hurt him badly and I won't be able to help. I see her and I feel completely helpless. If I could fly home tomorrow, I would—testing or no testing.

I guess Baba can feel my frustration because she

suggests meeting me at the pool. I shut the computer and go change into my suit. I invite Dad to join us but he's immersed in some book on quantum physics.

When I get to the pool, Mom is happily sunning herself while Marty is trying to stand on an inflatable raft. It's not working.

"Hey, Jade," he calls. "You'll never guess who we ran into on our hike."

"Who?" Then I pause. "Actually, I can guess. Les Crovley, from your class at school."

"How do you do that?" Marty says as I jump into the pool.

"Don't ask me—something about being one with the universe."

"Get one with this!" Marty says as he pushes a huge wave of water into my face.

"No, you get with this!" I call back and soon we're splashing and behaving like five-year-olds. Feels good.

I certainly don't want to think about Cindy, although her face keeps popping up. I shake my head and dive under the water, trying to get rid of the image. "You'll be home in less than a week," I tell myself. "There's nothing you can do from this far away. So forget it."

And I try.

# FIVE

We ARE ALL SITTING AT A DELI EATING THE early bird special. My favourite would normally have been the ribs or the chicken, except this psychic thing is now starting to interfere with my eating too. I can practically hear the cows screaming in pain and fright when they go to slaughter. I can feel the chickens all cooped together, pumped up with hormones. Actually, I'm not really sure if this has anything to do with my being psychic or whether it's Jon's influence, since he's a vegetarian. But whatever the reason, I'm eating fries and a veggie burger, which is surprisingly good, with a side of cheese blintz, which is amazingly good. Marty is deep into his ribs and pretty much in heaven. We are discussing our plans for tomorrow.

"You're going back there again?" Marty says, mouth full, meat spilling onto his plate as he talks.

I'm a little touched. He seems to want to hang out with me.

"I won't get this chance again," I explain.

"Oh, that's okay," he says. "Les and I want to go to this cool skate shop in Palm Desert and Mom says she'll take me if Baba doesn't mind going without the car again." He looks expectantly at Baba. She can never say no to us. She pats his hand.

"Of course, dear. I'll ask Leah to pick me up for bridge."

"Bridge again?" Marty asks.

"Almost every day," she answers. "Keeps us out of trouble."

"How long will you be tomorrow?" Mom asks me and Dad. "Maybe we can meet for lunch—the university and the skate shop aren't very far away from each other."

We agree to meet at a bakery where Baba says you can get the best pie in the universe, at noon.

We head back to the condo after dinner, stopping to pick up a movie on the way. As compelling as some old movie from whenever might be, I can't stay awake. I hit the sheets and am asleep right away.

~

# Far

*Mitchell and I are sitting on the bank of a pond. It's a lovely day and the birds are singing. As I look into the pond, the water turns black and I can't see either of our reflections. And then I'm drawn into the blackness. I can feel myself falling, falling, falling . . .*

~

I sit up with a start and swear. Marty, who is sound asleep in the bed next to mine, mumbles something but doesn't wake up. I flop back onto my pillow. What does the dream mean? Is it telling me that Mitchell is somehow bad? But I *fall* into the pond—he doesn't push or pull me. So maybe Mitchell isn't bad at all. Maybe something is after both of us. But how could that be? I just got here! I sigh. The last set of vivid dreams I had were more specific, actually showing me women who were about to die, but offering no way to find out who they were or how to warn them. My dreams are so frustrating! They seem to tell me just enough to worry me, warn me, whatever, but never enough for me to know what might happen. I'll definitely want to ask Dr. Black about that. At least now I have someone to ask.

The next morning, in the car, I tell Dad about my dream but he can't make anymore out of it than I can.

When we get to the campus we quickly find our way to Dr. Black's lab. Dr. Black gets me settled and we begin the testing right away. The pictures are different this time, a little more complicated to describe—like a child standing in front of an airplane or a mouse sitting in front of a cat—but I just say what I see in my head and it's all done soon enough. Dr. Black comes to fetch me and he has a huge grin on his face.

"You've done it again, Jade," he says. "Fantastic score!"

I can hardly believe it myself. Twice in a row has to be more than coincidence. Looks like I'm the real deal after all.

As I'm following Dr. Black out of the booth, another image hits me. Someone is in the small room I saw before. I can't see who it is, but they're trapped, screaming to get out. I stop in my tracks.

Dr. Black realizes I've stopped and he does too.

"What is it?"

"I'm seeing someone trapped in a small room."

"Did you see that while Mitch was sending?"

"No, just now."

"I think I know what it is. Come on, I want you to meet some people and then you need to have a talk with Mitch."

"I do? Why?"

"Best if he explains it to you."

We're in the front of the lab now and I realize it must be break time or something, because bodies are pouring out of the little cubicles. There are at least a dozen people there, some young university students, some older men and women, all in the middle of animated conversations.

"Everyone to the caf!" Dr. Black shouts over the noise and, ushering me and Dad out, he leads the way.

"Now, Jade, this is a good chance for you to meet some people who are very much like you," he says as we weave our way through the halls. "Today we had a big test going on—you and Mitch were just one of six pairs looking at the exact same images."

As he's speaking, a woman who looks to be in her late thirties comes up beside us. "Ah, Sonia," Dr. Black says, "I'd like you to meet Jade. She's here for a week on a visit from the frozen North and she's come to try to find some answers. Maybe you could talk to her."

Sonia has long brown hair that falls straight down her back and bangs over her eyes. She's no more than five feet tall, I'd guess, with a round face and huge brown eyes. She smiles at me. "I'd be happy to," she says. And then she shakes my hand. When she does that she stops for a moment and stares at me.

"Uh-oh," I say. "I know that look." It must be the way I look when I "see" something.

"It's nothing," she says. "We'll have a cup of tea and we'll talk."

Everyone sits at one big table in the cafeteria. Dad and Dr. Black sit near me—Dad on one side, Dr. Black across the table—while Sonia sits on my other side. I see Mitch at the end of the table. He waves at me and I wave back. I guess we'll get a chance to talk before we leave. Dad heads off to get me an iced tea.

"Did my dad tell you about the rock throwing yesterday?" I ask Dr. Black.

"He did."

Sonia jumps in. "Could you tell me what happened?" I do.

She sits quietly for a moment and then she says, "Jade, I know you've come here for help, but I need to tell you that something is wrong."

"That doesn't sound good," I reply.

"You have something upside down, that's all I mean. Or you will have something upside down."

And that's all it takes. Before I know it, my frustration comes pouring out.

"See, it's that kind of vague stuff that drives me crazy!" I exclaim. "I mean, I'm sure you're seeing something real, but what does it *mean*? Like last night,

I had a dream. I saw Mitchell and me falling into a black pond. But why? And why don't we see things clearly?"

Sonia laughs.

"I can totally relate," she says, smiling in a way that tells me she does. "But think about it. If we got direct messages from the 'other side' or from the universe, or from God, then God would be like a petty dictator and we'd be his generals. Everyone would have to listen to us because of our direct access. There would be no free will, no free choice, just us telling people what we saw and then them following our directions. I suppose it might be nice for awhile to be ruler of the world, but I can't see it being much good for anyone."

Dr. Black, who is listening intently, nods.

"She has a good point."

"Well, then what's the use of these 'powers' at all," I ask, "if it's stuff we shouldn't know anyway—if no one should know what the future will hold."

"Let me answer that," says an older man sitting beside Dr. Black. "I'm Nelson, by the way," he says and reaches over the table to shake my hand. "You're Jade, correct?"

I nod.

"Dr. Black told me about you and your results yesterday. Think about this. What if two things can exist at the same time? On the one hand, there's a way of knowing that we are used to—the way 'normal' people know things. On the other hand is a different way of knowing—the way that you know things and I know things and Sonia knows things. What if both of these ways are real? After all, reality is odd, isn't it? When you feel the sun on your face, you know it's real, even though you can't actually see the rays. You can't see a thought, but it's real too, isn't it? And your dreams have real information, but it doesn't come to you in the same way information in a newsletter would, correct?"

"No, you need to figure it out," I say, seeing his point. "But what if you figure it out wrong?"

"That could certainly happen," he agrees, "but at least you started with more information than most people do. Maybe you have a dream that you can think about, that might help you figure something out. Most people don't have that, so in a way, you have an extra ability—like super smell, or super sight, but it's super insight. It's just a bit extra, that's all. And you can use it to help others. Or yourself."

"Which she has done already," Dad puts in as he sits back down with my iced tea.

"I'd like to hear about that," Nelson says.

But I'm not ready to change the subject yet. This is interesting—no, it's *fascinating*—and I'm starting to feel like there might be a whole different way to think about my experiences. "I guess I can see what you mean," I say slowly. "I never considered what it would be like if I could see everything clearly. I only focused on how frustrating it is not to."

"What would the world be like if everything was fixed, preordained, fated?" Dr. Black asks. "There would be no point in anything."

"But if things aren't fated, what is it that I'm seeing when I do see clearly?" I ask.

"I suppose," he says, "you are seeing the most probable outcome."

"Or," says Sonia, "think of it like this. You decided to come to Palm Springs. You flew here. You could have taken the train. You could have driven, and if you'd driven, you could have come by a direct route, or by the scenic route. Your destination was fixed, but there were many ways you could have chosen to get here, and that's where our free choice comes in."

"But say you decide to drive," Dad says, obviously getting into this. "What if you have an accident on the way. You wouldn't have had that accident if you flew. Is that fated? Or is that part of your free will?"

"Think of all the things that needed to happen leading up to that accident," Nelson says. "All the decisions you made from the moment you were born, and all the decisions of the person you crashed into had to come together in a certain way at that exact moment to create that crash. I might call that fate, but others would say it was free will—that each of those decisions constituted a choice. Maybe it's all just how we name things."

"We're having a session tomorrow afternoon here," Sonia says. "Sort of like a psychic support group. Maybe you'd like to come."

I look at Dad. "I'd love to." These people have thought about so many things that have been troubling me.

He nods. I guess he can see that this is way more important to me than swimming or sun worshipping.

Just then Mitch comes over. "Could I have a word?"

"Uh, sure . . ."

He motions me over to another table a little away from everyone.

I grab my tea and follow him.

"Look, about the small room thing. . . ." He pauses. "My dad left my mom before I was even born." He pauses again. I feel a little uncomfortable. Why is he baring his soul to me out of the blue like this? His cheeks are pink, and he seems pretty embarrassed too. He takes a swig of his cola and continues. "The thing is," he stops. "When I was little, I was locked in a small bedroom for weeks at a time. My mom got sick

suddenly—she got cancer and had to have chemo—
and couldn't take care of me. To keep me safe she'd
lock me in a room with nothing in it so I couldn't hurt
myself. Ever since, I've been really claustrophobic. It
seems that whenever I open myself up to my psychic
ability that memory just floods back. Half the time I'm
not even aware it's there. That's why I was so freaked
out yesterday when you heard my thoughts, thoughts I
didn't even know I was having."

As he tells me this I'm seeing a strange sort of aura
around him—a kind of purple colour. I sometimes see
auras around people, especially when they are sick, but
I don't ever remember seeing purple and have no idea
what it means.

"I'm sorry," I say. "That must have been horrible."

"The sad thing is she meant well. She didn't want
me to go into care, you know? And eventually she got
better and everything went back to normal so I always
thought she'd done the right thing, but it was hard on
me at the time."

"That might explain what I'm seeing," I say, finally
getting it. "I had another flash today after we finished—a person trapped in a small room."

He looks almost scared now and his aura actually
turns dark, almost black. He seems to make an effort
though and sort of gives himself a small shake. His aura

gradually changes back to purple. "You're amazingly accurate," he observes. "Incredible for someone so young."

"I'm not that young!" I object. "I'm fifteen. I'll be sixteen this summer."

"I'm just eighteen," he says. "In my first year, taking psych."

I'm pretty sure he's blushing more than a little under those freckles. Does he like me? I take a swig of tea. "So, you going to this get-together tomorrow?"

He nods. "You?"

"I'll be there."

"Cool." He looks pleased.

"Cool."

Dad comes over then. "Jade, we have a lunch date."

Darn, just when things were getting interesting.

I get up, say goodbye to Mitch and to Dr. Black, Sonia, and Nelson. I tell them I'm looking forward to seeing them tomorrow. That's an understatement.

Dad and I walk out to the car, checking to see that the coast is clear. No problems this time.

"So," Dad says as we drive away, "are you starting to get some of those answers you're looking for?"

"Yes," I say, but I'm thinking about Mitch and can't help but be a little flattered that he seems to like me. Of course, he could never hold a candle to Jon, but it's kind of nice to be looked at that way by a university guy.

And then, suddenly, I get that flash again. A small room, but this time I can hear screaming and it's hard for me to catch my breath. . . . I gasp.

"Jade?"

"Nothing, Dad."

I must be plugged into Mitch in some basic way now. All I have to do is think about him and I relive his trauma! How weird is that? I make a mental note to bring this up at tomorrow's get-together. Maybe one of the others can help me understand what that's all about. Or maybe I'll talk to Mitch himself about it. That would be all right with me.

# SIX

I AM TUCKED INTO THE BEST OMELET I'VE EVER eaten, filled with avocado and cheese and tomatoes, when my cell goes off. I glance at it—a text from Susie. We can text long distance at no cost so that's how we've been keeping in touch if I can't get to the phone in our condo. I've let her know about the Cindy situation, in our shorthand.

"Disaster," Susie writes. "Check your wall."

I'm pretty tempted to check on my cell right then and there. Susie is so calm, cool, and collected, she never uses words like "disaster." Something must really be wrong. But Dad would kill me—the bill for going online from here would be brutal.

"What is it?" Marty asks.

"Susie—I need to check something as soon as we get home."

Mom shows me a very cool purse she found in a

little boutique while the boys were shopping. "There are some great shops here," she says. "Why don't we walk down El Paseo after lunch?"

Everyone else wants to, and although I'm dying to know what's going on at home, I'm also kinda dreading it, so I don't put up much of a fight. And we have a really great afternoon. The shops are amazing—cool clothes, art galleries, all interspersed with candy and ice cream places. We get this homemade fudge and ice cream that's beyond delicious. Mom buys me a summer purse and a very cool skirt and even Dad buys a shirt.

We finally arrive back at the condo around five o'clock and I log on to Dad's computer right away. What I find when I go to my wall takes my breath away—and not in a good way. No, it's more like the way that you can't breathe when someone punches you in the gut.

"Hey, Jade," writes Noreen, a girl in my class, "I heard today that you can predict the future. Will I have a good summer? Will Les and I still be going out in two months? Oh, and can you spell 'crazy?'"

"Ha, ha! No wonder you act so weird all the time. Do you hear voices? Never mind. I'm sure they're nice voices . . . ," Zach.

"I don't believe it," from Laura, a friend. "Lay off, guys! This is just a stupid rumour."

There's more, but I don't even want to look.

"Jade? Are you all right?" Mom asks.

I can't speak. I stumble into my room and slam the door.

Who talked? I mean, the only people that know are my family, Susie, and of course, one other person. Jon.

And who would he tell? He never would—would he? Not unless he was tricked or had confided in someone—someone who I already had bad feelings about, someone I knew was going to be trouble.

Cindy.

I'm shaking so hard I can hardly pick up the phone. Mom opens the door. "Jade?"

"Not now. I need to make a call."

She looks really worried, but I have no time to make her feel better. I sit on the bed and dial Jon's number. It'll be almost seven thirty at home, so he should be there.

He answers.

"Hey, how'd it go today? Another triumph?"

"Jon, I need to ask you something and I need you to be honest with me."

"I'm always honest with you," he says and I can hear in his voice that he doesn't appreciate the implication.

"Have you seen Cindy again since the poetry slam last night?"

"Actually, we met for an hour after school today at

the coffee shop. We went over a couple of scenes from old Julius and talked about her poetry. I'm trying to encourage her to write more."

"Did you talk about anything else?"

"Like what?"

"Like me."

"Only that you and I are going out and that you're away right now and once you're back I won't have as much time to spend with her—we'll just stick to the two sessions a week."

"But did you *tell* her anything about me?"

"Jade, what's going on?"

"Are you near your computer?"

"I can be, just a sec. OK. What?"

"Go onto my wall."

There's a pause.

"Oh no . . ."

"Oh yes." And then it finally hits me and I start to cry. "I'll be the laughingstock of the city, never mind my school." I pause. "Why did you tell her?"

"What do you mean?"

"I mean what I said. Why did you tell her?"

"Jade, are you *crazy*? I didn't tell her!"

I'm so mad at him I can hardly hold the phone. "Well, no one else knows! You, me, Susie, my family . . . I mean, you must have. There's no other way."

"Look, it might seem that way but I would never—I hardly know her! She's not even a friend. Not that I would tell a friend. I've never mentioned this to anyone—not Liam, not Brendan, not Maria, not one of my best friends. Why would I tell *her*?"

"You ignored me about Cindy and my feelings and now this has happened and I just can't see that it's a coincidence. I don't blame you for not admitting to it, but you might as well."

There's a long silence. "I feel horrible for you," he says finally. "And I'll do whatever you need me to do so I can help. But you have to drop this idea about Cindy. And about me. You can't trust me at all if you think I'd betray you like this."

Now the silence is on my end.

Maybe I do have it all wrong. For a moment I feel quite chastened. Why shouldn't I trust him? He's never lied to me. He's always been straight. But how else could it have happened? Nothing else makes any sense, especially after all my bad feelings about her.

I hear Mom call, "Jade, supper."

"I have to go," I say. Not that I do. I'm not that hungry—no surprise—and I never pay attention to Mom calling me to dinner anyway. But I want to phone Susie and see what she's heard. Maybe she can tell me how this all started. Maybe she can trace the first posting.

55

"Jade, don't hang up like this."

"I'll talk to you later," I say. "I need to go."

I hang up and dial Susie, my hands still shaking.

"Hi."

"Jade, I didn't tell anyone, I swear."

"Of course you didn't," I say. "I just accused Jon."

"He wouldn't!"

"How do you know? He and Cindy are such good pals now. It would be easy to let it slip, wouldn't it? And then how could he admit it to me?"

"Jade, that's just not Jon. He could never be so . . . so . . . careless with such a big secret." She pauses. "What did you say to him?"

"You don't want to know."

"That bad?"

"That bad if it's not him. But I still think it is."

"Well I don't."

"Then who? And how do we stop it?"

"I'm already on the stopping it thing," she says. "I've organized Jason, Patti, Morris, and Leah. We're all posting rebuttals on our walls and on yours as well. By tonight it'll just seem like a bad joke. That's what we're saying—that it's just a joke. You need to go on, too. Don't protest too much. Make a laugh out of it. In fact, say it's all true and you predict the Bisons will win the season—you know, stuff like that, just funny."

Susie is amazing. She always jumps in whenever there's a problem and solves it before the rest of us even realize it's there.

"You seriously think I can bluff my way out of this?"

"Of course I do! After all, who's going to believe it? They might for a few minutes—I mean, they might believe *you* believe—but most of them would never accept that you could be a real psychic."

"That's true!" I exclaim. "You're right. We can beat this! I'll post right away. It'll be okay, right? Right?"

"Yes, it will. I promise." Susie never makes a promise she can't keep.

"Jade, before you go . . ."

"What?"

"What's the deal with Jon? You don't really think it was him, do you?"

I sigh. Susie's like a pit bull. She never gives up if she has something in her teeth and she's not letting up on me and Jon.

"Okay, I guess I would never have jumped to that conclusion if I hadn't had this awful feeling about Cindy and I saw all this black around her. There's something very, very bad connected to her. Maybe this is it."

"Listen, after the thing with my mom, far be it for me to question your 'feelings,' but are you sure this is what they are about? Maybe Jon's in some kind of danger and instead of being mad at him you should be trying to figure out what it is."

"If he told her about me, then I don't care what happens to him!"

"You don't mean that!"

I sigh again. "Not even close."

"Be prepared to grovel if you need to."

"I don't think it'll be me grovelling. But hey, thanks for this."

"What are best friends for? We'll have this squashed in no time."

We hang up and I venture out into the living room. Baba has arrived and everyone is sitting at the table eating. Mom has made a big salad and put out a cold chicken from the supermarket. They all look at me expectantly.

"Someone's posted on the Web that I'm psychic."

"What do you mean, posted?" Baba asks.

"You know that page I showed you?"

She nods.

"There's writing all over my wall—mean jokes about me being crazy because I think I'm psychic."

Everyone starts talking at once and I can hear how upset they all are. It's not so much what they say, but I can feel the emotion coming off Mom and Dad and

Baba. Even Marty seems pretty shaken. They want to protect me, of course.

"Susie has organized a counter-campaign," I say. "She wants me to go online and make light of the whole thing. She thinks we can cut it off."

"You go ahead, darling," Mom says. "I'll make you a salad and you can eat it later."

I put Dad's computer on the coffee table and log on again. "Kids can be so cruel, can't they?" Baba says from the table. "But maybe you shouldn't correct them. You could help people if they knew. They could consult you about things."

"Don't you think she has enough on her plate right now, Mother?" Mom says. "She needs to concentrate on her school work and try to live as normal a life as possible. She doesn't need to be giving 'readings' to every kid who has dating trouble."

"There are far more serious problems than dating," Baba objects, "as you well know. High school is a tough time for so many, and Jade could help."

This is all happening as I am reading the wall. Added onto the messages I've already read are comments from my friends. They all say that this is a ridiculous joke and that no one should pay any attention. Someone with the username "gossipguy" seems to have started the string, but there's no way to know who that is. It could easily be Cindy, pretending to be a boy.

I add my own comment.

"Just read about my amazing super powers! Wish someone had told me sooner! Could have predicted the long cold winter, the horrible holiday concert (how bad was that, anyway?!). Oh, and I could tell you for sure that the Bisons will win their season despite all evidence to the contrary. Feel free to check back with me for all your psychic needs!"

I hit send.

Within minutes there are thirty replies. And most of them are of the "yeah, this is too funny" kind.

I post once more, then email Susie to thank her. Her strategy seems to be working.

"So?" Dad asks as I finally close the computer. "Fire out?"

"I think so."

"Any closer to finding out who started it?"

I think about Jon. "Not yet."

"Come and eat something," Mom says.

I go to the table and sit down. If Jon was telling the truth he might never forgive me. If he wasn't, I might never forgive him. I look at my food and realize I have no appetite. I get up and go out to the patio, where I sit alone in the dark. And feel sick.

# SEVEN

I HAVE A BAD NIGHT, AND IT DOESN'T HELP THAT Marty seems almost more upset about the web stuff than I do. Every time I try to put it out of my mind I catch fragments from his—like "Oh no, this sucks, this is so bad. . . ." I'm sure he's worried about what this means for him, and I can certainly understand. I mean, having a crazy sister will put him in the direct line of fire from kids who want an excuse to pick on him. School's a jungle and the weak don't do so well.

Mom and Dad decide over breakfast that we're all going for a hike. Then we'll come back to the condo for lunch. After that, Dad can drive me over to the university while Mom and Marty hang out at the pool. Marty is trying to see if Les can come over and join him. Dad, meanwhile, has arranged to meet a Math professor from the university while I'm at my meeting.

We drive into Palm Springs, right to the very edge

of the mountain, to a trail Mom discovered in her hiking book. We park on the street and put on our packs, which are stocked with water and snacks. Dad has his cell with him, just in case, although Mom says there's no way we can get lost. This trail climbs up in a winding path and eventually goes all the way to a museum, but we won't go that far—we'll just turn around and come back when we start to get tired. It's rated easy to moderate.

There's one little problem: the trail splits right at the start and we're not sure which path to take, but a friendly young woman starting up the trail with her dog asks if we need help and then points us in the right direction.

Dad leads the way with Marty following him, then me, then Mom. As we walk, Dad tells us what the trees and plants and cacti are called. Some of the creosote bushes are thousands—yes, thousands—of years old. That's so weird.

The trail isn't crowded but we do pass people who are on their way back—a jogger, another woman with a dog, a family of about six who aren't carrying any water and look like they are about to pass out. This gets Mom going: "What's the matter with people, don't they realize this is the desert and you can die out here without water?" And on and on. It's hot today, that's for sure, and the heat seems to rise up from the dirt and the rocks, making it even hotter.

I turn to gaze at the view and catch my breath, letting Mom pass me. Quickly the entire family has moved around a curve in the path and for a blissful moment I'm alone. I step out onto a small shelf and look down at the city and across the valley to the mountains all around. It really is stunning. I think how I can describe it to Jon later when we talk and then stop myself. I might never get to have another conversation like that with him again. I can feel tears burning at my eyes. How could things have turned so bad so fast?

I hear someone coming around the curve from where Mom just disappeared and I figure it's her, doubling back to find out what's keeping me. I start to turn, ready to call her over to look at the view with me, but I don't get the chance. Before I can even fully turn my head, I'm pushed from behind. I have no time to see who's pushing because I'm at the edge of the cliff and I'm lurching forward. I grab at the bush beside me and use it to stop my forward momentum while simultaneously throwing my weight back. I end up sprawled on my rear, still hanging on to the branch. From what seems like very far away, I hear my mom call, "Jade, catch up, please."

I can't find my voice. I'm gasping for air and sitting on the ground, unable to move. Mom rounds the corner.

"Jade!" Instantly she's on the ground beside me. "David, come back," she yells.

"Are you all right?"

I nod.

Marty shows up next and then Dad.

"What happened?" Dad asks.

"Someone pushed me," I say.

Dad has his arm under mine and is helping me up and drawing me back from the cliff edge.

Mom says, "Did you say someone pushed you or pushed *past* you? A jogger running really fast just raced past us."

"What did he look like?" I ask.

"He had a hood on," Dad replies. "Couldn't see his face at all."

"I don't understand," Mom says. "Do you think this was on purpose?"

"I don't know." I shake my head, confused. "Maybe the person was running fast and got round the curve and lost balance or couldn't slow down and just barrelled past me, not even realizing he'd really pushed me."

I see Dad looking at me. He knows I'm putting the best face on this so Mom and Marty won't freak out. But it's not working, at least not with Mom. I can tell she's about to argue with me, so I throw her a look and then glance at Marty. She catches on.

"You're right, that must be it," she says.

"Maybe it's a serial killer who kills his victims by pushing them off mountains," Marty suggests enthusiastically. So much for protecting him. "Boy, you were lucky, Jade!"

"I don't think it was luck," I say, "I think it was my ballet training. I was able to catch my balance—most people would have pitched right over the edge."

Mom sits down hard on a rock. Dad puts his arm around my shoulder. "Time to head back?"

That would be the natural thing to do, but somehow I don't want to. If this was on purpose, why should I let the maniac ruin my day?

"Let's keep going," I say.

Dad nods in approval. "But no lagging behind, I think," he says.

I fall in line behind Dad with Marty behind me and then Mom. We do look out down the trail when we reach higher points to see if the jogger is still around but if he is we can't see him. Then it occurs to me that it might not even be a he. It could just as easily be a she.

I follow along and let Dad point out the patches of wildflowers, purple and yellow and gold, the cacti that look like fuzzy mounds—Dad says they are called teddy bear chollas—and the views around every curve. We stop often to appreciate the views, and bit by bit my heart rate slows and I start to really think about what just happened and how close I was to hurtling over the edge to my death. Is it a coincidence that two days in a row I've had a close call?

Still, who on earth would want to hurt me? It's not like I have any enemies here. Who would even know I was on the mountain, for heaven's sake—Mom and Dad just chose the route this morning! So it *has* to be coincidence. I try to home in on the person who pushed me to see if I can get a feeling, but I can't seem to catch anything at all.

We stop at a natural resting spot with rocks to sit on. We drink water and I munch on a granola bar. Dad says he thinks it's time to start going back.

"I think we'd better report this to the police, just to be on the safe side," he says.

"I'll do that while you and Jade go to the university," Mom offers. "That way you'll still get your afternoon out."

"Yes, and who better to ask about this than a group of psychics," Dad says. "Maybe someone will be able to see something you can't, Jade. You've often told me that it's harder for you to see things that relate to yourself, correct?"

"Correct," I agree, my mind jumping to Jon and Cindy.

We make our way down the mountain with no trouble, and once at home, I go straight to the computer to see what's happening with my online status as an All-Star Freak.

My wall is filled with comments like, "Jade, please tell me the answers to the pop quiz in Math today," and "Jade, some people are so nuts they don't even know they're nuts, but you aren't one of them," and "Hey Jade, whoever started this is the real freak." I smile. Susie rules. She can do anything.

I email her right away and then text her too.

She answers instantly—must be in between classes—and says, "Victory is ours!"

"Need to find culprit," I text back.

"U R so right."

Just as we sign off I remember Morris's friend Robert, a computer nerd of the first order. If anyone can dig up the real person behind gossipboy, he can.

I text Morris, who texts me right back. He'll ask Robert and let me know as soon as he hears anything.

Relieved, but still worrying about Jon and Cindy, I head off to get changed and ready for my afternoon with the psychics.

# EIGHT

A SIGN SAYING "GET TOGETHER!" AT THE entrance to the second floor lab points me and Dad to a room down the hall. We open the door to find a room painted all in bright blue. There's a large table in the centre with refreshments on it, and chairs all around the edges of the room. The get-together is already in full swing, with people sipping on punch and eating nachos and dip. Dr. Black motions me in, excusing himself from a tall, lanky fellow with huge glasses.

"Hello Jade, hello David," he says, shaking Dad's hand.

"Hi Nathan." Dad smiles at Dr. Black. "I've arranged to meet Marvin Lesky from the Math department in the cafeteria. Will it be all right to leave Jade here for an hour or so?"

"Absolutely." Dr. Black smiles. "We'll take good care of her."

Dad looks at me to be sure I'm still okay with it,

after the morning and all. "I'll be good, Dad," I assure him. "No worries."

I see Mitch in the corner talking to the departmental secretary. He waves me over.

"I'll just go talk to Mitch," I say.

Dad waves goodbye and takes off.

Mitch seems genuinely happy to see me. "Hey Jade! Have you met Chrystal? Sounds funny—Jade meet Chrystal."

We smile at each other. "I like your name," we both say at the exact same time. Then we both laugh.

"I think you two might be on the same wavelength, or should I say mining the same territory."

We both shoot him a look.

"Fine, I'll stop right there," he says grinning.

"How do you like working here?" I ask her. "Are you psychic too?"

"Not a bit," she replies cheerfully, "and just as well. They need someone who can organize everyone and never has to worry about getting feelings or flashes or hunches."

"Organizing is its own special ability," Mitch says. "Take it from someone who can't do it!"

"I hear you two had some amazing results," she says.

"Yeah, I wanted to ask you about that," I say to Mitch. "Why do you always act as a 'sender'? Don't you also get psychic feelings? Or are you just really good at sending thoughts?"

"I do get psychic flashes," he answers, "but I seem to have this ability to communicate well with others. It just comes naturally to me."

He smiles at me and I can see he's not boasting. There is something so easy about his manner, so disarming. It's clear he has somehow tapped into that and made it special. Just as I'm thinking that happy thought I get another flash of the small room. I hear screaming, and I flinch, just a bit.

"Jade, are you okay?"

He's sharp to have noticed anything.

"Fine. I'm fine."

"Want to get some air? We could go out to the quad and sit in the sun for a few minutes."

He's including both of us in the invitation, but Chrystal says no. As much as I want to talk to the others, I suddenly really need some fresh air and sunshine. I nod.

"I'll just tell Dr. Black where we'll be," he says. "Wouldn't want him to worry about you."

He pops over to where Dr. Black is standing. I see the professor nod and then we head out. Sonia looks over at us as we make our way out, and her brow furrows. I make a note to talk to her as soon as we get

71

back. Mitch finds us a spot on a bench under a large olive tree. I sit down and sigh. The shade is glorious, much better than his initial suggestion of sun. It's really hot out here in the afternoon. There's a lively hum around as students talk to each other or on their cells.

Mitch plunges right in. "The reason I suggested we come out here, away from the group, is I can feel something from you, Jade. Something's wrong. Want to talk about it?"

His adorable freckle face looks so open and kind, and his blue eyes crinkle up in a smile that says I can tell him anything and it won't end up on the Web.

I spill. I tell him about what happened on the trail, and he's so sympathetic that I end up telling him about the Internet thing and then everything else, too. And although all he does is listen, I feel better.

"You're amazing," he says and I can feel my cheeks getting hot. "First of all, you're brave. I mean, no falling apart on the mountain, no hysterics. You save yourself and carry on. And the thing with your boyfriend? I think you were easy on him. I mean, you warned him to stay away from her, didn't you?"

"Yes!" I exclaim. "I did! That's what's so maddening. It's not like I'm wrong about these things. Something about her is all darkness and he should have listened to me." I pause. "I know he'd never hurt me on purpose, but she could have wheedled it out of him, and then he'd be ashamed to admit it, wouldn't he?"

"Still, you have someone tracking down the culprit, right? I'd wait to see what turns up before I said anything else," he says.

"Getting anymore flashes about the small room?" he adds.

"I just had one a few minutes ago."

"I've been thinking about it," he says. He puts his hand over mine. It's warm and dry. He only leaves it for a moment and then takes it away. "I think the sending and receiving we've done over the last couple of days has created a connection. Like a new wiring or something."

In a wacky, weird way, that sounds totally romantic to me. I want him to put his hand on mine again.

"Anyway," he says, "what do you think? Make sense?"

"It does, for sure," I say.

"Want to take a walk?" he asks.

"Sure."

We stand up, ready to leave the quad, when Dad and another man appear out the door nearest us.

Dad makes his way over and introduces me to Dr. Lesky. There's a pause. "So what are you two up to?" he asks. I can see he's wondering why we aren't upstairs.

And I can feel he's thinking he didn't bring me here just so I could hang out with Mitch. Mitch must feel it too.

"We're just going back upstairs," he says.

Dad nods and watches us until we're in the door.

"Parents," I say with a small embarrassed laugh.

"They try," he says, taking my hand and giving it a squeeze. We go up the stairs and into the room and as soon as we're inside Sonia comes and catches my arm.

"Can we talk?"

"Sure."

She pulls me over into a corner away from everyone.

"Jade," she says, "I don't know why, but I'm getting stuff about you all of a sudden. If you don't want to hear it though, just let me know."

"Of course I want to hear it," I say and something in my stomach turns over. I can feel it's not good.

"Let's get you something to drink first," she says, and I wonder if she's picking up on my nervousness. She guides me over to the table and pours me some fruit punch. As I'm waiting, I overhear an older woman saying, "And I could see the body in the ditch, and I could see all this detail, except I had no idea where it was. It was so frustrating!"

I don't want to be rude to Sonia, but I just have to

get into this conversation—it's one of the reasons I so badly wanted to meet other psychics.

"Excuse me, but what do you do when that happens?" I ask, interrupting the woman's story. "And why does it happen? Why can't we see more clearly from the start?"

The woman turns to me. "You must be Jade. I'm Maureen, and you're asking the right person. I've been at this my whole life."

I wait.

"And?" I say.

She pats my arm. "I have no idea, my dear," she says, laughing. "In fact, your guess is as good as mine."

"I don't even have a guess," I say.

"Well, here's the thing," Maureen says. "I work with the police all the time. Now it's true that in the case you overheard me talking about, I could only describe what I saw. But the police had a suspect who lived in an area without sidewalks, just gullies along the streets, and they had a closer look at this fellow because they know my information is very reliable. Sure enough, they were able to find forensics that tied him to the crime. So together—their facts, my intuition—we put a killer away."

"And is this the way it normally works for you?" I ask.

"Yes. I rarely get a name—although I have—but I often get enough to give the police a clue that's vital."

This is a revelation to me. Suddenly, it makes sense. I can see that I don't need to be perfect, that I don't need to always see clearly. What I *can* see is still important. It can still matter. Maureen must notice the look on my face.

"What I just said made sense to you, didn't it?" she says.

"Totally," I say.

"That's why we have these support groups," she smiles.

I can feel Sonia at my side, so I thank Maureen and excuse myself. We walk a bit away from the others and Sonia finds a chair. I sit down beside her.

"I had a dream about you last night," she says softly.

"Really?"

"Really. I dreamed there was a dark shape hovering around you, and the more you moved the more the shape morphed into you until you and the dark shape were one."

"Nice."

"Jade, something is wrong."

"Can I tell you what's been happening?" I ask.

"Please."

For the second time this afternoon I spill my guts

about the weird accidents and about the Internet "outing" and about Jon.

Sonia listens and takes my hand for a moment. Second time today that's happened too. "It's like I said yesterday. It's all upside down. What you think is up is down, and vice versa."

"So I have something wrong?" I say, wondering where to start. The accidents? Jon? Cindy? It could be anything.

"You've heard about optical illusions?" she says.

"Yes."

"It's like that. Everything seems to be one way, but it's quite the other. You know how you can never truly see your reflection in the mirror because right is left and left is right? That makes it impossible to see yourself exactly as you are. Reality can be like that too. A small tweak and everything looks different. You have people in your life that you can trust and you have to believe in them. And you have to believe the universe is worthy of your trust as well."

What? I start to wonder if Sonia is some kind of religious case. Is this about her trying to convert me somehow to something?

She laughs. "I'm not a missionary," she says, reading my thoughts. Psychics! "Trust is a funny thing, Jade, and the person you need to trust the most is yourself."

"But how can I do that when you've just told me I'm getting everything wrong?" I ask. And I know I sound a little sulky.

"I never said it was easy," Sonia says. "Find a place inside you and fill it with love, and then use that place to help you think clearly. I know it sounds corny— even flaky—but it will work. You'll know things in a way that simply feels true. And you need to do that now. This thing I can feel—it can be stopped, but only if you can see more clearly, if the blackness doesn't take you over."

And then I suddenly get the flash again—the small room flash—and Sonia grabs my hand. "What was that?"

"What?" I say, stunned.

"I felt something, I could hear screaming . . ." she says.

I need to make a split-second decision. I've already told Dr. Black about the images of the small room— and I know they are about something private in Mitch's past. The last thing he needs is more people in his head, right?

"It's nothing, really. Just something I've been feeling since I got here. I've told Dr. Black, and he's not worried about it at all."

She looks at me for a moment.

"In this business," she says slowly, "we need to learn

to trust ourselves, as I told you. But we also need to get to know ourselves, because if we fool ourselves we can't see things clearly."

Now she's freaking me out.

"What do you mean?" I ask. "How am I fooling myself?"

But before she can answer I see Dad waving at me from the doorway, his meeting obviously over.

"I need to go," I say.

I look at her hoping for an answer, but she shakes her head. "I'm sorry, Jade. If it were clearer I'd tell you."

I look around the room. There are so many more people I should meet, so much else I could learn. I'm going to have to collect email addresses before I go home.

I say goodbye to Sonia and she squeezes my hand. I get up, go over to say goodbye to Dr. Black and he steers me toward Dad.

"Jade, I want to ask if you'd be willing to do more work here before you leave? And David, I don't want to spoil your holiday, so just say if it's too much."

"I'd love to," I answer immediately. I look around the room and catch Mitch's eye. He flashes me a big grin.

"I think the family should do something together tomorrow," Dad says. I'm about to object when he adds, "but Friday morning should be fine. In fact, I'd like another chance to meet with Dr. Lesky and some of his colleagues, so maybe we could set that up for Friday, too."

Fair enough, I think.

"Actually, David, if you aren't in a rush I'd like you to meet someone. His name is Ben Cross and he's a mathematician who's also a psychic."

"Sure," Dad says, as Dr. Black steers him across the room.

My cell goes off just then—a text from Susie. "Fire! Fire!"

"Oh, great!" I mutter.

Suddenly, Mitch is beside me.

"What's up?"

"Not sure yet," I say.

I text Susie back. "Where? What?"

"More n yr page. U R being tested. How know that?"

I look up at Mitch. "Someone's posted that I'm here being tested. It's one thing to post the psychic thing, but no one but Jon, Susie, and my family know about the testing."

Mitch shakes his head. "I'm so sorry, Jade. You deserve better."

I'm furious. I'm so mad that I'm not even upset

about what a disaster my life will be when we get home. I'm too busy thinking of all the evil things I want to say to Jon. I say as much to Mitch.

"Don't be too hard on the guy," he says. "He probably felt like he could trust this girl."

"Trust her? He doesn't even know her!"

"I hardly know you," he says, "and I know I can trust you. Maybe he just made a bad judgment call."

The nicer Mitch is the madder at Jon I get. How could he betray me like this? And why?

I text Jon. "Seen my page lately?"

"We might be working together again on Friday," I tell Mitch, shoving the phone into my pocket.

"That's great!" he says. "I'll look forward to it. When do you go home?"

"Saturday."

"Too bad," he says. And he touches my hand with the tips of his fingers.

"I'll see if I can get back and visit my Baba again next year," I say quickly, trying to cover how discombobulated I am by his touch. "Especially if Dr. Black can arrange some more tests and things." I add this last bit so I don't sound like a dopey kid.

"Even if he can't you should come back," Mitch says.

I'm so pleased to hear him say that I can't think of a thing to say in reply.

My cell goes off and I pull it from my pocket, then glance down at the text. It's from Jon. "Didn't come from me. I swear!"

Before I can reply, or even tell Mitch, Dad comes up. "Ready, Jade?"

"See you Friday," I say to Mitch.

"Not the end of the world, remember that," Mitch says and gives me an encouraging smile.

I'm not so sure.

# NINE

Jon and susie are sending me texts by the minute all the way home. I tell Dad what's happened.

"Look Jade," he says, "I know it's not looking good for Jon but don't you owe it to him to give him the benefit of the doubt? I mean, he's telling you outright that this didn't come from him, and Jon has never struck me as a liar. If he were, Mom and I would never let you go out with him, especially as he's so much older."

"It's hardly your fault," I say, "if he turns out to be a creep."

"Yes, but Aunt Janeen sees him almost daily now that she and Sahjit are moving in together. And she dotes on him. She's told me that she thinks Jon's one of the finest young men she's ever known—takes after his father, naturally."

"Well, there you go! She's a little prejudiced," I answer.

"So were you until yesterday!" he exclaims. He pauses. "Does Mitch have anything to do with this?"

"What do you mean?"

"Just that maybe you wouldn't be so quick to dismiss Jon if you weren't getting some attention from a very nice-looking university boy."

For a split second I admit to myself that Dad's hit on something. Then I push that thought out of my head and jump to my own defence. "No way! I saw something about Cindy, I warned Jon, and he thought I was being jealous!"

"And you're sure you weren't?"

"Whose side are you on, anyway?"

"Yours, Jade. Always yours."

We ride in silence the rest of the way home, and once inside, I race to the computer and log on. And there it is: another post on my wall saying that my abilities are being tested in Palm Springs at some university. And more posts from kids in my class, some starting to take the whole thing seriously again, some just joking.

I post that my dad is here meeting with people at the university and that this whole thing is stupid. I add a line about how whoever is posting this stuff should have the nerve to post under his real name or shut up.

That last bit gets lots of support. And all my friends are on the site, sticking up for me. I call Susie.

"Any luck finding out who's doing this?" she asks.

"I hope Robert's still working on it. Meantime, I'm thinking I should just stay here with my Baba. My life won't be worth living once I show up at school next week."

"Not true! After all, half the kids here don't know who you are anyway."

Good old Susie. I have to chuckle. "That's true."

"On the other hand, they might know you now. This thing is spreading like crazy."

"Great."

"Hey, we'll make it through this. Have you talked to Jon?"

"Not today. Well, only texts."

"Why?"

"What am I supposed to say to him? I'll accuse him again and he'll deny it again and we won't have anything else to talk about." I pause. "I've met this guy."

"What???"

"No! I mean, we're just working together and he's testing with me but he seems to like me. He's in first year."

"And so, what? You like him?"

"Why shouldn't I?" I reply.

"You tell me."

"Well," I say defensively, "there's no reason at all I

shouldn't like him. He's cute, he's understanding, he 'gets' what it's like to have abilities and to be different, he's been super cool about the Jon and Cindy situation . . ."

"Hold on. Hold on! You told him about that?" Susie sounds shocked. "You told him you're having trouble with your boyfriend?"

"So? And, I mean, it's hard to avoid considering he's psychic. He knew something was wrong."

"Jade," Susie says, "be careful."

"I'm not stupid, you know!" I say, annoyed despite myself. Susie only wants what's best for me, I know, but she's not here, she hasn't met him, she shouldn't judge. "I mean, I only see him at the lab—we're not dating or anything."

"But maybe this is why you're blowing Jon off."

"I'm not calling Jon because I'm mad at him. Period."

"Okay, okay. If you say so."

I sigh. "Yeah, my dad said the same thing. But honestly, I don't know what to say to Jon. I'm sure precious poet Cindy somehow wheedled all this out of him."

"Say you're right about Cindy," Susie says. "I don't get why she'd want to 'wheedle' anything out of Jon. What would be the point?"

"The point," I say, "would be to find out my weak spots and then use them against me to steal him!"

"Can you say 'insecure'?" she chides me.

"I can say it, but that doesn't mean it isn't happening. Like, just because you're paranoid doesn't mean people aren't out to get you."

Mom pokes her head into my room.

"Come on, Jade, we're leaving."

We're going to the deli again for dinner so I have to say goodbye. Part of me is relieved—I don't like where this conversation is going.

Once at the restaurant we spend dinner trying to figure out what to do with our free day tomorrow. Baba suggests we go to Joshua Tree National Park.

"It's so beautiful there and you can hike and then go to the outlet stores on the way back."

"Shopping! Sounds good to me," I say. There's something else, too. I have a feeling—a feeling that we should get out of town tomorrow.

# TEN

My sleep is filled with strange dreams. In one, Marty is sitting on a rock, saying he's sorry over and over. In another, Jon is crying. That almost breaks my heart. And then there's one where a dark cloud hovers over the university and gets lower and lower until it smothers all the buildings until they melt.

I wake up in a sweat. As I eat breakfast I try to figure out what it all means, but as so often happens I basically have no clue. I'm just left with this distinct feeling that something is wrong—very wrong. I mean, dark clouds smothering things can't be good. After breakfast we head off, leaving Baba at home as she doesn't want to slow us down on the hike.

The bad feeling left over from the dreams won't go away. Once in the car I try to shake it off but instead of decreasing as we drive, the feelings increase. I'm sensing something, I'm not sure what, a kind of dread now, and it's building and building until it suddenly takes a shape I can latch onto. It's something to do with the car and our drive. . . .

Just as we're about to turn onto the road that will take us to the highway, I tell my dad to pull over—quick!

Dad has pretty fast reflexes for a guy his age and he pulls right onto the shoulder. We're barely off the road when a car barrels out from a side street, swerves and speeds away—narrowly missing us. Mom gasps.

"Good one, Jade," Marty says.

"What was that?" Dad gasps.

"Just a feeling," I answer.

"Any more?" asks Dad.

"Yeah, I think going out of town is a good idea today," I reply.

"You amaze me, Jade," Mom says as we continue on.

I'm wondering if this near miss was another accident avoided or something worse. I'm sure Dad and Mom are wondering the same. Mom told me that she reported the push to police but they were pretty unimpressed. Since they'd had no other reports like it, they were sure it was just a kid running too fast. But three "accidents" in a row? Still, there seems to be an unspoken agreement not to dwell on it, but to try to have a nice, "normal" day.

As we drive into Joshua Tree National Park, about a forty-five minute ride from Palm Springs, Dad explains how the famous bushes got their name. Being Dad, he'd looked it all up last night before going to sleep. Anyway, they are these incredibly shaped trees—all twisty and gnarled—and, according to Dad, a member of the lily family. When Mormons were travelling through the area on their way to the town of San Bernadino in the 1850s, they saw these amazing trees and thought they looked like Joshua calling them to the promised land. The Mormons called them Joshua trees, and the name stuck.

The park is up at high elevation, and the desert here is cold compared to the weather in Cathedral City this morning. Fortunately, because of Dad's research, we all brought sweatshirts. We stop at the visitor's centre and buy a guidebook and a map and then head off.

We make our first stop at a group of rocks that look like they've been carved, but it's just erosion. One looks like a skull, one looks like a seal, another like an elephant. It's amazing. We take lots of pictures with Marty and I posing in front of the rock formations. I camp it up, but Marty isn't his usual exuberant self. It's like he's just going through the motions.

We get back in the car and drive to a trail that apparently has the best view in the park. We stop for a moment to stare at a coyote that is standing by the road staring at us. I know they are carnivores and not dogs to be petted but I think they are really beautiful. As we continue driving, Dad names off plants he recognizes from his studying last night—yucca plants, ocotillo, smoke trees, cholla. Anyway, we arrive at the parking area and get on our gear. It's a pretty steep path up and Mom looks a little leery. I can sort of see why. This hike follows a rocky trail, complete with steps made from rock, and is quite different from the dirt path we were on the other day. And it doesn't look easy. Marty and I start up in front of Mom and Dad and pretty soon we're well ahead of them. Mom and Dad don't freak about this, though, probably because the path is pretty straight, and they can still see us.

At a lovely lookout I sit down on a rock and Marty sits on another and we gaze out at the desert and mountains around us, waiting for Mom and Dad to catch up. Man, it is beautiful! So peaceful and quiet and calm. I take a deep breath and let it out slowly, feeling some of the tension drain out of me, and that's when, suddenly, I know that something is very wrong with Marty. I can "hear" him saying, "You have to tell her, you have to tell her," over and over to himself.

"Tell me what?" I ask.

He glares at me. "I hate it when you do that!"

Just then we're interrupted by a shriek from below. We peer down the trail and see Dad hovering over Mom. She must have tripped.

Dad looks up at us and waves that it's okay, but it looks like they are going into her pack—always prepared, Mom brings bandages everywhere and of course has hand sanitizer with her at all times.

Dad is yelling to me but I can't hear him. I make a gesture like, "What?"

He signals back that we should wait where we are. So we settle back onto the rocks. I zip up my sweatshirt as the wind seems to be picking up. The sky is such a clear blue and the view is so amazing—filled with wild flowers and cacti and palms and Joshua trees, and of course the valley below and mountains in the distance—that for a moment I forget there's something Marty needs to tell me. But only for a moment.

"Okay Marty, spill. What is it?"

"You're going to kill me."

Now I'm really interested.

"Then it must be pretty important. Tell me."

"First you need to promise not to kill me."

"I'm not sure I can promise that," I say.

He looks terrified.

"I'm kidding! What?"

Mom staggers onto the plateau then, swearing a

blue streak and favouring her knee. Dad is right behind her.

"Look what I did," Mom says and shows us a really nasty gash on her knee. It's got three little bandages over it, but isn't completely covered. Some blood is still oozing out. "I tripped going up one of those stone steps," she says. "Hurts like . . . well, it hurts."

It really does look ugly.

"I think this is as far as we should go," Dad says. "We can drive to the rustler's caves in Hidden Valley instead."

This would normally be the part where Marty would jump in and say "cool," but he's totally quiet. This time, Mom notices. "Marty, you can't be that worried about me falling down. You've been off all morning. What's the problem?"

"He was about to tell me," I say. "Apparently, it's something I'm going to kill him over."

"Can you tell us too?" Mom asks.

She's all about privacy and not needing to know every little thing her kids do.

"You'll know soon enough," he sighs. He's staring out at the view, refusing to make eye contact with any of us. "Okay, remember when I met Les and we went shopping?"

"Yes," I say and suddenly there's this black cloud. I

can see it, it's settling over me, and the image is so strong that I look up to be sure it's in my mind and not actually there.

"So, we got talking and we were just telling each other what we were doing and he was boasting that his family was here because his sister was going to get into UCLA and she had been there for an interview and it was on scholarship and so I said that was nothing, that you were here being tested for being a psychic."

For a moment this doesn't compute. I just stare at him.

Mom reacts before I do.

"Marty, you realize how wrong that was, don't you? How much this will hurt Jade? And how it's already hurt her with Jon?"

"I'm really sorry," Marty says. And now he is looking at me. "I'm really, really sorry. As soon as I said it I knew I'd goofed up big time, but I was hoping Les wouldn't repeat it or he'd forget or he'd think I was making it up, but he thought it was really cool and he started asking about how Jade was psychic so I ended up telling him about the murders and . . ."

I leap up. Now I will kill him. "You didn't!"

Marty nods miserably.

"Jade, sit down," Dad says. "Marty, you have to try to make this right."

"How?"

"You need to tell Les to go back on to Jade's wall and say that he's been kidding."

"But that would be asking Les to lie," Mom objects. "And even to help Jade that can't be right."

"Well, at least he can promise not to say anymore," Dad says. "He hasn't posted about the murders has he?"

"No," I say, "He must be saving it. He's posting something new every day."

"Yes," Mom says, "that's because it makes him something of a celebrity."

"Has he posted other stuff about other kids?" I ask.

"Yes," says Marty. "He's the 'gossipguy.' It's what he does. But I didn't know he was 'gossipguy' or I never would have told him," Marty assures me. "I just figured it out when gossipguy's post told everything I'd told Les."

"So he won't want his cover blown."

"For sure not," Marty agrees.

"Then you need to tell him to stop or you'll tell everyone who he is."

"He'll be mad," Marty says.

I glare at him. "If he wants mad, I can show him mad!"

"Okay, point taken. I'll text him now."

Marty texts Les and we all wait to see if he gets a reply.

He does.

"No prob. No more on that. Don't give me up."

Marty texts him back, promising that he won't.

I shake my head at him and start down the mountain ahead of everyone, my mind racing. Jon. What have I done? And what was the black cloud around Cindy if it wasn't this? What a mess!

# ELEVEN

I SIT IN THE CAR IN A DAZE. AFTER DRIVING FOR a bit we get out and go for a smaller hike in Hidden Valley, where cattle rustlers used to brand not only their own cattle but those they stole as well. I hardly take in anything, though, and Dad's monologue about history falls on deaf ears. I am trying to think of ways to make this up to Jon, but my mind keeps blanking. And I *still* don't understand the dark cloud business. What if there really is something dangerous about Cindy and I've ruined our chances of finding out because now Jon won't trust *me*?

I sit down on a rock and text him.

"Sorry! Not Cindy! Not U. Sorry!"

I put my phone back in my jean pocket and wait for it to vibrate. Nothing. Finally the hike is over and we're back in the car heading for the outlet stores. We're all starving by the time we get there, and the first thing we do is grab some lunch at one of those all-day breakfast places. I'm feeling the need for major comfort food so I order pancakes and eggs and muffins and stuff my face. Mom and Dad chat about the park and how beautiful it is and everyone basically leaves me alone. Marty knows better than to even try to talk to me. I mean, I know he was doing it because he's proud of me, but how immature can you get? Didn't he realize what would happen to me at school if this got out? And what might still?

After lunch Mom suggests that we split up and meet later. Dad and Marty can go to manly shops and we can go to our favourite name-brand stores. I was so excited about this before—all the places I like to shop with the same clothes at, like, half the price. Now I couldn't care less.

"Come on, Jade," Mom says. "It's called retail therapy."

And I have to admit that once inside the first shop I do get caught up. It's a way to forget everything, and Mom needs help—she's got the worst taste ever. By the time we meet up with Dad and Marty I am actually feeling much better. Mom has a cool new blazer, a new bag and new shoes, and I have three new tees, a new pair of sneakers, two pairs of shorts, and a summer sweater, all for the price of one pair of sneakers at home.

# Far

Before we leave the outlet stores we stop at Hadley's—famous for their dates—and stock up on dried fruit, and we each try a date milkshake. Awesome.

On the way home, we go to a take-out place and pick up tacos and burritos and fajitas and chips. I get the veggie version with beans and rice. After we eat, I take the phone out to the patio and call Jon.

He picks up. I thought maybe he wouldn't.

"Hi, Jade."

"Hi."

"So who was it?"

"Marty."

"*Marty?*"

"It wasn't Marty that posted. It was Marty who told a friend from school who he met out here and this kid posted."

"And he took this long to tell you, even though he knew you were blaming me?"

"Younger brothers. He was scared."

"I don't blame him."

Pause.

"Jon, I'm so, so sorry. But there *was* this black cloud around Cindy and everyone's always telling me to trust myself, and I saw this so . . ."

This sounds lame even to me.

"But that doesn't explain why you didn't believe *me*, does it?"

It's what I most feared him saying.

"No."

Another pause.

"I don't know where we go from here, Jade. I just don't know."

"I don't blame you," I say. I don't want him to hang up but there's nothing clever I can say to stop him.

"I'll be home on Saturday," I say.

"Have a safe trip."

"Thanks."

I hang up the phone and then sit there staring into the dark.

Disaster. He's beyond mad. He thinks I'm immature and he thinks I don't trust him. The thing is, a bit of me still doesn't trust him. I mean, what's the thing with Cindy, anyway?

I call Susie. I tell her what's been happening.

"So what did Jon say?" she asks, and thankfully doesn't say she warned me.

"It couldn't be worse. He's beyond mad. He's calm. He's reasonable. And I don't think he's going to forgive me." I start to sniffle, feeling very sorry for myself. "I was only trying to protect him."

"You can't really blame him though," she says. "You'd

react the same way."

"I know, I know," I say. Why can't anyone see *my* point of view? Even Susie, who knows how real my visions can be.

"Did you grovel?" Susie asks.

"Pretty much."

"You said you were sorry, but is that all you did? That's not grovelling!"

"Well, maybe I don't want to grovel! Maybe I'm still right about Cindy! Who knows what those two are up to?"

"Jade! No way! Not Jon!"

"How did Jon suddenly become this saint?" I ask. "You should have heard my dad talking about him!"

"Yeah well, I should be so lucky, love-wise," Susie sighs.

"So what's the latest online?" I ask, taking a deep breath and changing the subject. "I don't even want to look anymore."

"You know, it could be worse. I think mostly everyone thinks the message was some sort of prank. I mean, you'll probably get a bit of hassle from the usual suspects, but nothing you can't handle with some jokes. Pull a Jon Stewart. Agree with everything they accuse you of and exaggerate it even more. Say yes, you're the greatest psychic on earth, etcetera,

etcetera—like you did on your first posts—and that should work."

"Hey," she adds, "the weather is finally changing. The snow is melting like crazy."

"Thanks for everything," I say. "I'll try to call you tomorrow. Otherwise, we're back Saturday around five."

"See you then," Susie says. And she means it literally, I know. She'll be over within minutes of my return.

When I go back inside Mom, Dad, and Marty are all watching some old action movie on TV. I put Dad's laptop on the table and log on. It's not too bad, although it's not great either. I can see the first week back will be pretty miserable, but I have no choice but to get through it somehow.

I don't want to watch the movie so I tell Mom and Dad I'm going over to Baba's. I haven't seen her all day and maybe she needs company. Okay, I'm the one that needs company, but whatever.

She's delighted to see me. Even if it's been only five minutes since she last saw me or Marty, Baba acts as if it's been years.

"Jade, sweetheart! Come in!"

"Were you busy?"

"Reading."

What else?

"Are you hungry?"

"Not a bit," I say.

"Are you sure? Some dessert maybe? Some cheese-cake?"

"Well, if it's cheesecake."

In no time she has me sitting at the table with a giant slice of cherry cheesecake and a cup of mint tea. She takes a sip of her own tea. "All right. Tell me everything."

I laugh. Feels good, too—the first time I've laughed all day.

Baba always knows when I need to talk. So I go over the whole mess with her. She knows all about the psychic stuff and even helped me at the start, when I couldn't accept the new ability, by introducing me to one of her friends who's psychic.

When I'm done she leans over and kisses me. "Don't be too hard on yourself, darling. We all make mistakes. Even Jon will make his share, don't worry."

"But I seem to have messed everything up and gotten everything wrong," I say.

"You're talking like it's all over—you got 'everything' wrong."

I'm not sure what she means.

"I did!"

"Everything isn't over, sweetheart. You're still in the middle of it all."

"Huh?"

"Life isn't like a movie, is it—where there's one main story or episode that is told and then it's over. You're still in the middle of all of it."

"Yeah, but there are episodes in life, and this thing with Jon might turn out to be just that now—something in my past."

"But it doesn't have to be over."

"I think Jon's already decided. I don't think he can forgive me. I don't think he wants to."

"And you can't make him. But maybe when you figure out what the black cloud around Cindy was all about, he'll understand."

"So you believe me, that there was—is—a cloud."

"Of course I do! But what is the cloud? Are you seeing it clearly? Fear is a terrible thing. It makes us do terrible things."

"Fear?"

"Fear."

I'm not sure what she means. Baba is usually so easy to understand.

"Eat your cheesecake," she orders me, before I get a chance to ask her anything more.

I do. And it is delicious.

"Now, my suggestion is that you get a good night's sleep and just let things come to you. Don't push it, but don't cloud your mind with worries or excuses for how you've behaved. Be open, be relaxed, and it will all sort itself out."

I get up and give Baba a big hug. And I leave with that wonderful feeling that even if I were an axe murderer Baba would love me anyway.

When I get back to the condo Marty is in bed, the light out. Guess he didn't want to face me. I change and do my teeth in the bathroom and then crawl into bed too. We're due at the university at nine.

~

*I am at the university. The sky is full of clouds and Mitch and I are on the roof, picking out different shapes in the clouds. One of the clouds becomes big and black, and Mitch turns into Jon. The cloud gets lower and lower and falls onto me and then I'm the cloud. Jon is yelling at me to get away from him but I'm getting closer and closer and finally I touch him and he gets drawn in and he's screaming. The screaming turns into a girl screaming and someone, I think it's Mitch, is saying, "You can stop it, Jade, you can stop it!"*

*"How? How?" I scream.*

*"Cindy. She's a poet and she doesn't know it."*

*"That's just stupid," I yell.*

*Everything is black now and I can't see anyone. I can only hear their voices and the screams.*

*Baba says, "You* can *see Jade. It's not black. You* can *see."*

*And then the black starts to dissolve and there is a light so bright I still can't see because now the bright light is blinding me.*

*But through the light I can sense something and then Zaida is there! Standing right in front of me, clear as day, just the way he did when I almost died. And he says, "Don't be afraid. I'm here, Jade. Do what you need to do. I'm here."*

I sit up in bed.

What was that?

# TWELVE

For some reason, maybe the dream, I wake up in the morning filled with dread. Marty keeps his head under the covers and doesn't venture out while I'm still in the house. Probably a good idea.

I eat a piece of toast and some jam and drink some OJ. Then I put on a pair of my best jeans and one of my new tops—shades of pink that go surprisingly well with my red hair.

I'm still feeling awful about Jon but a little bit of me is thinking, so what? I've got another guy in the picture now, and he's also cool and cute, true, not drop dead-gorgeous like Jon, but very adorable—and he's into me, I can tell. Let Jon disapprove of me, let him drop me even. Who cares?

I'm looking forward to this morning and to being with people who understand me. People who won't make fun of me. People who get me.

Still, I'm thinking about that dark cloud around the university. Wonder what on earth that could mean?

I'm never much good at conversation first thing in the day so it's a pretty quiet ride to the university. Dad takes me upstairs, says hi to Dr. Black and then takes off. He's all excited because Dr. Lesky has set up a meeting with three other mathematicians. They're getting together over at the faculty lounge and Dad won't be back to pick me up until lunch, so I'll have the whole morning in the lab.

Mitch is in already and so is Chrystal, who is going over a schedule with Dr. Black. I can see some others in the glass booths, too.

When Mitch sees me, he comes up and says, "Hi. How's everything?"

"Okay." I look up at him. "You were in my dream last night."

He grins. "Were we frolicking through the flowers?"

"Not exactly."

"Nothing bad, I hope?"

"I don't know," I say.

"Well, let's grab a coffee at break. You can tell me then."

"Sure, I'd like that."

Dr. Black comes over then and Mitch takes off for

somewhere, giving me a backwards glance that I can't quite figure out. He looks worried all of a sudden. He looks. . . .

"Now, Jade," Dr. Black interrupts my thoughts, "we're going to do something different today. We've devised an experiment where various psychics will all read the same person or subject. In this way, we'll be able to see how many 'hits' each psychic has. For instance, will all of you pick up on similar things? We'd like you to have a crack at it—three others have already had their turn. In fact, we have two subjects for you to read, if you think you can manage it."

"You mean I'm going to give a reading, like someone in The Chocolate Shop?"

"The Chocolate Shop?"

"It's a place at home where people pay to get readings."

"Just like that."

"But I have no clue how to do that!"

"That's interesting to us. You've never practiced this. You aren't in it for the money, as a business, or just altruistically to help people. You aren't 'in it' at all. That makes you very valuable as a test subject." He pauses. "You can imagine the difficulty we have here, making sure we remain a legitimate part of the university. We are dedicated to investigating phenomenon such as psychic ability with scientific rigour. But how do you scientifically test something that you can't see?"

"How *do* you?" I ask. "I mean, before this happened to me, all I wanted to do was be a scientist. I didn't believe in anything other than science and facts. That's why it's all been so hard for me to accept."

"Many scientific experiments deal with things we can't see," he continues. "We posit based on certain ideas. You can't see subatomic particles, but you can see how they behave. We can't see dark holes, but we can measure them. So what does seeing really mean? You, for instance, see things that most people can't, but this doesn't mean those things aren't there. We're trying to measure the unseen, so to speak."

"That makes sense," I say.

"So will you try?"

"What do I have to do?"

"We'll put you in a booth. For ten minutes you'll just sit quietly and tell us anything you get on the subject. You won't see him or her. The subject sits quietly in the other side of the booth, the way Mitch did during the sending experiment. After ten minutes I'll tell you that you can start to talk directly to the subject and get a bit of feedback—yes's or no's. After the reading is done we'll have a transcript and a video, and we'll add up all of your hits, all the things you say about the subject that are accurate, and compare them to what the other psychics get."

"Okay."

"Ready to start?"

I look around to see where Mitch is, but he's gone. I wonder if he'll be my subject.

As usual, Dr. Black takes me to the booth and gets me settled. I sit there in the absolute quiet and wonder what's going to happen. Will I get anything right? Maybe it'll turn out that I'm just a dud. And that would be all right. I wouldn't mind going back to the old me. I mean, maybe the dark cloud with Cindy *was* just my imagination, and maybe all of this will leave just as fast as it came on and I'll be me again. Scientist me. Egghead me. The me I know and love.

Suddenly I get an image of a waterfall. Standing by it is a young girl, maybe ten or so, and she's holding hands with an older woman with blond hair in a pony tail. I say all this. Silence. I guess this is the ten minutes where I just say whatever I see. Now I see the woman with the pony tail and she's poring over books with signs and symbols in them—I say aloud that I see her reading astronomy or something. I see lots of stars. I see an older woman with her. The woman is sick, though, coughing and pale.

Nothing much else comes to me and finally Dr.

Black tells me I can start asking questions. I ask if the woman with the pony tail's name is Karen because I keep hearing Karen in my head. And she says, "Yes." She sounds calm but I can hear in her voice that she's not; she's excited because I've somehow made a direct hit. And then I ask if her mom is sick and she says yes, and I say it's something in her lungs, and she says yes, and then I know her mom is going to die and I say that too. I feel bad, but I see it. And then I don't get anything except I know Karen is crying. Finally Dr. Black says, "That was great, Jade. Can we try one more subject? Would you like a break? Would you like something to drink?"

"Some water would be good," I say, suddenly feeling very thirsty.

He comes in with a glass—no plastic here I've noticed—and puts it down.

"I did well, didn't I?" I ask.

"You look unhappy about it," he replies.

"I was almost hoping I wouldn't," I answer. "Hoping it would all just go away. And it's not great when you make people cry."

He looks at me sympathetically and pats my shoulder. "I know that can't feel good," he says. "But we need to play the hand we're dealt, Jade. That's the way it is with all of us. I could have had a much more traditional career filled with honours and awards. Instead, I'm at the fringe of my profession."

"The fringe or the cutting edge?" I smile at him.

He smiles back. "That's certainly what I'd like to believe. Ready for more?"

"Yup, let's go."

A moment later I hear Dr. Black's voice saying, "We're starting the ten minutes, Jade. Just sit quietly and tell us whatever comes into your head."

But what comes into my head isn't so much a picture as a feeling, and that feeling is a sudden, brutal headache. I actually say "ow" out loud.

"What is it?" asks Dr. Black.

"Headache."

There's a pause. "You've got that right. Just realize it isn't yours, it's the subject's, and it should go away."

I do as he suggests and sure enough it starts to recede. I close my eyes. The quiet is absolute. And then—there's Zaida!

"I see my Zaida!" I exclaim.

Zaida takes my hand. "I'm here with you Jade," he says. "I'm here."

"I'm so happy to see you," I answer. But Zaida doesn't look happy. He looks so serious. As if he's worried for me, or trying to reassure me or something.

"What is it?" I ask.

"I'm here for you, Jade. Ask me when you need to. I'll help you." Did he say something like that in my dream?

And then he's gone and instead of him I see the small room and hear screaming.

"My Zaida is gone and I see the small room again," I say. "Is Mitch my subject?"

"I can't tell you who it is," Dr. Black says. "Just tell me what you see."

"I see this small room. Mitch is there."

There's a pause.

"Is this what you saw before with him?"

"No, it's different."

"Jade, open your mind. See what else you get. It sounds very much like you are tapping in to his childhood trauma. I'm not passing this information on to him yet, just in case that's what it is."

I try to do as Dr. Black suggests. I open up to this image. And then, suddenly, horribly, Sonia's words come back to me, shouting inside my brain for no reason at all. "You have everything upside down."

Why am I thinking of this now?

I don't have time to sort that out before I hear Zaida's voice again. "Dark clouds, that means something."

Am I losing my mind? In the silence of the booth I

remember my dream and the dark cloud, but what does any of that have to do with Mitch? None of it makes sense! I try to focus my thoughts on the dark cloud to see if anything comes to me. The cloud hovers in my mind and then descends onto me, as it did in my dream. And now I hear Dad saying, "Are you sure you aren't jealous?" I know this has nothing to do with the reading I'm supposed to be giving and I'm worried that I really shouldn't be thinking about this now, but I need to know what it means! I let my mind follow and the dark cloud becomes me, just like before and then suddenly I gasp.

"Jade? Are you all right? Is the headache gone? You haven't said anything for a bit."

"I'm sorry, Dr. Black. It's a dream I've been having and I haven't been able to figure it out and it's really vivid right now."

"This happens sometimes," he says. "It's the quiet of the booth and the time alone. I should have warned you. Often psychics get things unrelated to the subjects but related to their own life. Just go with the flow."

I do. I sit with the cloud and let it slowly seep into me. And then, all at once, I know exactly what the dream meant all along. The black cloud was *me*! The black cloud was my jealousy! The black cloud was me worried that I wasn't good enough for Jon and that he'd realize it and as soon as he found someone better he'd drop me. It was me, convinced that this would eventually happen because I was just a freak with all this weird psychic baggage, and he was just perfect.

Tears come to my eyes as I realize that what I feared the most I made happen.

"I'm such an idiot," I whisper.

"No you aren't," Dr. Black says.

I remember that this is all going on tape.

And then something in the pit of my stomach turns over as Sonia's words ring in my ears.

What else have I gotten wrong?

# THIRTEEN

"Jade?" it's dr. black's voice.

"Yes?"

"Mitch has asked for a break—I think you've already figured out he's your subject—so let's take a rest. When you come back we'll do one more session with the two of you. I'll set it up a bit differently."

I am happy for the break. I'm thinking maybe I can confide in Mitch and he'll understand. And it's consoling that although I've probably blown it with Jon, Mitch still seems to like me.

Mitch gives me a big warm smile when we get out of our booths and suggests we go to the student lounge for coffee. Dr. Black tells us to be back in a half hour. As we walk Mitch tells me that the lounge is on the other side of the campus but it's nice and quiet compared to the cafeteria. He must know I need some quiet after the last session.

"Sounds great," I say. "Man, that stuff takes it out of you. I don't know how psychics do it all day! I'd die of exhaustion."

"They learn how to pace themselves, that's all," Mitch says. Then he adds, "Hey, would you like to see something neat?"

"What?" I ask.

"I have a friend who's set up a painting studio in the basement here," he says. "We have to go that way anyway. Want to check it out?"

I hesitate. A little voice says, no, you don't want to go into the basement.

"She's very cool," Mitch assures me, before I have time to pay attention to that voice. "She's having her first show at a big gallery in Palm Springs next week and we can look at all her paintings before they go up. Come on—we'll only stay for a minute. She's so nervous about the show I promised her I'd drop in."

"Sure," I agree. After all, if he's being so nice, trying to prop up a friend, who am I to get in the way?

I follow him down the stairs and through a large basement door. The place reminds me of the basement in *Buffy the Vampire Slayer* where all the weird things happen. This one is well lit though, and doesn't seem to have any crazy monsters popping up out of the sewer drains. We walk down a wide corridor lined with utility rooms and then take a turn down another hall. The voice in my head is getting louder, basically telling me to run. And since the last few days have been all about trusting my "feelings," I decide I'd better pay attention.

"Hey Mitch, I'm getting a bad feeling down here," I finally tell him.

He stops dead. "Really?"

"Really."

"Well, your bad feelings are usually right. Maybe we'd better go back up."

I'm so relieved. It's great that he trusts me.

"Look, her studio is just up here. Why don't you go ahead and get our drinks—I'm pretty sure I can give you directions you can follow—and I'll meet you there." He reaches into his pocket and pulls out some cash. "Here," he says, offering me some bills.

"Put your money away," I say. "I have enough for a couple teas. How do I get there?"

"Okay. You keep going with me, take a left at the next turn, no wait, a left at the second turn . . ."

I grin. I feel silly suddenly. "This is crazy!" I say. "I'll just go with you. That way I won't get lost and need a search party sent out for me."

"Yeah, that would not be cool," he says. "To be known as the girl who got lost in the basement of the university."

He's making a joke and we both laugh, but there's something in his laugh and his expression that I just can't catch. He seems off somehow. . . .

"So, shall we continue on or are we doomed to be eaten by sewer monsters or something?" he asks.

"Carry on," I say, feeling really silly now.

We walk for at least another full minute before he says, "Just up here." "Just" is actually about two more minutes of walking and now I'm starting to feel a panic rise up in me. The hallway is totally deserted and the only sound we can hear is the sound of our footsteps. Mitch has gone quiet, which is strange, but I don't know what to say to him either. I realize I don't know him very well and here I am, alone with him in some crazy maze. I'm just about to say, "no more" when he motions to me. "Right here," he says and points to his right. There's a steel door propped open with a piece of wood. Mitch motions for me to go ahead of him and calls out, "Hey, Lorrie, it's me! I've brought my friend, Jade."

And then, everything happens very quickly. As Mitch is talking, I'm peeking through the door. But I don't see any paintings, and I don't see Lorrie. What I see, mostly, is nothing—white walls, a small room, an old table with a few files on it and some old coffee cups. I'm about to tell Mitch that we have the wrong room when suddenly, sickeningly, I see the room for what it is—the room from my visions. I know I need to get out of there, and get out fast. *Danger*, *danger*, the words are screaming at me. I turn to tell Mitch we have no time to lose. I see him bend over and catch at the piece of wood. He snatches it up, and in a smooth movement removes it from the door with one hand while pushing me into the room with the other. The door slams shut behind us with a mighty clang.

For a moment I don't understand what's happening and I stand staring at Mitch. "What?" is all that manages to come out.

I can see sweat break out on his forehead.

"What the hell?" I exclaim.

I push past him to open the door and see, to my horror, that there is no doorknob. There is no way at all to open the door from the inside.

I am so stunned that I'm actually at a loss for words. I just don't get what is happening.

"I've set up a test," Mitch says to me.

"Huh?"

"I've set up a test," he repeats.

It's still not making sense.

"You've what?" I finally speak.

"I've set up a test. I couldn't tell you, you would never have agreed. Sorry I had to do it this way."

I start to get it—he's planned this.

Stay calm, I tell myself. There has to be a way out of here. He's a claustrophobic person—he wouldn't deliberately lock himself in a small room. Would he?

"Let's just hope you're as good a psychic as you seem to be," he continues.

I'm trying very hard not to panic, not to freak out. "Mitch, please explain. I'm scared."

"I am too," he assures me. "I'm claustrophobic! But this was the only way to set up something and still be able to explain it away in case you got into my mind and sensed that something was wrong. And you *did* see the small room. You even saw me in it. But I was able to explain it to you and you bought it, so the plan worked." He looks around, dread replacing the pleased look in his eyes. "Still, now I'm not so sure I'm going to make it through this."

"Mitch! Please! The test?" He's almost babbling now. Inside I'm screaming at myself for not listening to my instincts. I could have easily said no when he asked me to follow him down here. I knew I should have said no. But I trusted him. And more to the point, I wanted him to like me. I didn't want to come across as a young high school kid. No, I have to admit now that I wanted him to see me as possible girlfriend material. Saying yes seemed to be the way to do that.

"I'm telling you!" he continues. "I timed an email to be sent out," he checks his watch, "at exactly 10:30 a.m., four minutes ago, telling Dr. Black and Chrystal and everyone on my psychic network list that I'd be taking you to a secret location and that they will have to find us before our air runs out. I've also emailed CNN and the *Desert Sun* so the media can follow what happens. I did it as soon as Dr. Black said we could go on break."

"I still don't get it," I say. "Follow what? What are you trying to do?"

"All the jokes and teasing and shrinks—my life has been miserable thanks to my so-called 'abilities.' No one really believes. Sure, Dr. Black is doing his best to take away the stigma, but he's so rigorous and his studies take years to publish—it's way too slow. So I figured out this plan. So simple. I lock myself in a room and the psychics have a few hours to find me. If they don't I die, and that's okay because I'm sick of living like this, and if they do then I'm famous and rich with book contracts and people coming to me for readings and no more ridicule. When I came down here to look for a place to stage my experiment, I found this room—the university must be have built it as a freezer, with the steel door and everything—but it's not in use right now."

I am so blown away by the craziness of what he's just said that I don't know how to react. I try kicking at the door but only hurt my foot doing it. Finally I turn to him and say, "But why include me? To be suicidal is one thing, Mitch, to be a murderer is another. If we're not found we both die, and even if we make it out, you've kidnapped me, so you won't be famous, you'll be in jail."

"That's true," he agrees. "But when you came along I couldn't resist including you because you are so strong in your abilities and the chances of actually being rescued and vindicated are way better. Also, I realized that no one would really care about me. So what? Some kid locks himself in a room. It might not even make the news. But if I take a high school girl with me, well, the media loves stories like that."

"So this really isn't a suicide mission, is it? You *want* to live. You *want* to be found. Even if it means jail?"

"I was thinking maybe I could figure out a way not to go to jail—that maybe I could say I was crazy."

"But you're doing this so people will see that you aren't crazy." I'm yelling now. "Which is it?"

He shrugs.

I stare at him. And then it sinks in. He is crazy. Really crazy. And he's done this for who knows what reasons. Probably none of them will make any sense.

Maybe he does want to die. Maybe he doesn't want to die alone, so he brought me. Maybe he's doing this is instead of jumping off a bridge or shooting himself. This way, he can trick himself into believing he's doing something in the name of science, that he's proving something.

And then something else sinks in. I'm in trouble—deep trouble. There's no way out of this room. Yes, people will be looking for us, but will they find us in time? I start to scream and bang on the door. "Help! Help! In here! In here!"

And then I realize something: the person I heard screaming in the small room was me.

# FOURTEEN

"No one will ever hear you through a steel door," Mitch says, his voice calm and reasonable. "And you'll use up all of our air. We should both start sending our location out to people. That's the only way we'll be found."

But I don't trust my abilities the way Mitch seems to.

"It doesn't work that way!" I protest. "I can't just communicate with anyone, mind to mind, at will. You know that! It's so hit and miss. I can't even understand it myself. That's why I came here—for help! And man, was that a mistake." I pause. "Come on, Mitch! Think about it! If I was so brilliant I wouldn't be stuck here, would I?"

"You did have a bad feeling, you just didn't listen to it," he says.

"How long have you been planning this?" I ask.

"Ages," he says. "The fact that I work with psychics made it really hard. I needed to plan something I could mask as part of my own life, so I took my claustrophobia and used it."

I stand in the tiny white room and think about Sonia saying I had everything upside down. "I liked you. I trusted you. I never had any inkling, for instance, that you'd been bullied or harassed or anything like that. So that must make me a pretty bad psychic."

"Actually," he says, "you're not as bad as you think. I've become an expert at fooling people. I've learned how to block myself off from others trying to read me—for the most part, anyway. I have to let my guard down during tests and experiments, though, which is why you got the small room pictures. So, you aren't bad. I'm just practiced at blocking." He pauses for a moment. "Don't you think we should get to work?"

"I hope you have a Plan B if this doesn't work."

"No," he says, "no Plan B."

I take a breath and try to focus, but I'm too panicked and afraid. My breath comes out shaky and I'm trembling all over. Mitch puts his knapsack on the table and fishes out a bottle of water. He hands it to me.

"Don't suppose you brought your computer?" I ask him.

"Just water," he says. "A few bottles. We'll run out of air eventually, but there's no use being dehydrated, too."

"How long do we have with the air thing?" I ask.

"I'm not exactly sure, but I asked a friend of mine in science and he figured that a room this big with two people would hold enough air for about four hours."

I look around the room. "But what about the vents? The room must be ventilated?"

"I've blocked them off," he says, looking up.

I follow his gaze and see that there are vents on the walls, maybe reachable by standing on the table. There are boards across them. That might not make them airtight, but maybe it would. What do I know?

Staring up at those vents seems to do something to Mitch. He goes pale and sinks to the floor. "I don't feel so well," he says.

"That's because you're an idiot!" I yell. I know I should be nice to him—who knows what he's capable of?—but my temper gets the better of me, as it often does, and I see red. "You can't stand small spaces, but you've got us trapped in here. You've brought us water, but cut off our air! Mitch, how could you? You've met my dad. What will happen to my family if I die? This will destroy them! Did you think for a second about anybody but yourself? What a selfish pig!"

I am so angry that I kick over the lone chair in the room, wishing it was him. He isn't that much bigger than me, I think, wondering if I can take him on if I need to. I figure I probably can. But he doesn't seem to want to hurt me—outside of the killing me part.

"Look," he says, "you can throw your little tantrums or you can do what you're here to do and concentrate on sending out an image of where we are. We need someone to tap into it and find us before it's too late."

I give the chair another kick before picking it up and sitting down. I glare at him. "Aren't you going to do it too?" I ask. He's leaning against the wall, sipping his water and taking deep breaths. It crosses my mind that since he's horribly claustrophobic he should be having some kind of panic attack or something and yet he isn't.

"Are you on anything?" I ask.

"Just a tranquilizer," he answers. "Anti-anxiety pills I take for my claustrophobia. I carry them all the time. I took two to be on the safe side. If they don't find us in time I'll give you some," he assures me. "Then you won't be scared."

"Oh, that's really thoughtful of you," I say, my voice dripping with sarcasm.

"Aren't *you* sending to people too?" I repeat. "You're probably better at it than I am."

"I doubt I could send anything with all these drugs in me," he answers.

"Oh, that's brilliant," I say. "So now you've halved our chances of succeeding."

"Maybe I didn't think it through as well as I could have," he concedes, "but whatever, you'd better get started."

All I want to do is hurt him, so it's very difficult to get into a calm state, one where I can concentrate. And yet, I need to and I need to do it fast. I close my eyes and try to block him out. I take a few deep breaths and focus. I create an image in my mind of exactly where we are and try to send it. I send it to Sonia and Nelson especially, because they are the ones I've had contact with and they might actually get the message. And when I do this for awhile my mind seems to calm down and in that quiet I see Zaida again.

"Zaida!" I say. But not out loud.

"Jade, I wanted to warn you. I tried to. But sometimes thoughts can't get through. I'm not sure why."

"Well, your thoughts are coming through loud and clear now."

"Either my thoughts or your own dressed up as mine," he answers.

"Jade, you may have to hit Mitch."

"What?"

Carol Matas

"You'll need air. You might need more than four hours to get out of this. You might need to knock him out long enough to pull down those boards and let in some air."

I think back to the self defence courses I took with Mom. I know how to hit hard, right on the jaw. Preferably with that piece of wood he left lying on the floor.

"I don't want to hurt him." I send the thought to Zaida.

"You need to live," he says simply.

I sit with my eyes closed. What if I kill Mitch when I hit him with the board? How could I live with that? I don't know what to do. I picture the room again in my mind and concentrate on sending out pictures. And hope someone will find us before I need to choose.

# FIFTEEN

I'VE BEEN SITTING QUIETLY FOR ABOUT FIVE minutes, eyes closed, when I suddenly get a flash of Mitch running, wearing a dark hoodie. I open my eyes and stare at him. "It was you?"

He knows what I mean.

"I tried to get you away from me. Tried to warn you off—first the rock, then the push. I didn't mean to push so hard, really. I didn't want you to go over the edge. And swiping your car that day? I followed you to the condo. It's not hard to get in if you sneak in after another car raises the gate. I thought maybe I'd get you hurt or scared enough to keep you away, but when nothing worked I realized it was meant to be—you were meant to be part of my plan, the one sacrificed. Or the one to save me. One or the other."

Now I'm really, really scared. He's been trying to hurt me for days. And I had no clue.

And then I hear Zaida again. He says, "Tell him his mom is sorry."

"My Zaida is telling me to tell you that your mom is sorry."

"You're talking to the dead now?" he asks. He seems surprised and a little skeptical.

"Apparently."

"What does she say?"

I listen. And instead of Zaida I actually hear someone else. A light female voice.

"She says that she was just trying to keep you safe, but that she was wrong. She says you need help."

He shrugs. "You could be making this up."

I wish I were making it up, in a way. This is all I need. More weird powers! But the voice is quite insistent. I listen some more. "She says you had a favourite toy she would put in the room with you. A teddy called . . . Bruce? Bruiser?"

"A teddy called Brubru," he says, eyes opening wide with surprise. "No one knows that. Only me."

"She's saying something about how we relive the pain we cause others when we die, and that you won't want to feel the pain you'll cause me and my family. She says you need to get us out."

"She's saying I'll go to some kind of hell?" Mitch asks.

Her words are coming through like a little kid's voice on the phone—fast and thin and not quite understandable. "I think she's saying that there is no hell. Only the hell you make. And that you need help from the same people you hate. They're the only ones who can help you."

"Are you making this up?" he accuses me. "You could have read my mind about the teddy bear."

"I wish I was making this all up!" I say. "I've never talked to dead people before, it's kinda freaking me out."

"What else is she saying?"

"That we need to get out of here." I wait, but I don't hear anything else. I start to think again about how we can get out.

"Why did you take the knob off?" I ask Mitch. "Is it here somewhere?"

"No. I knew if I left it in here I'd crack and let myself out," he answers. "I filled in the hole where the knob was with putty and sealed it."

I see red again.

"You're such a little coward," I say, fiercely.

"Excuse me?"

"You heard me! You weren't trying to warn me off when you did those things, were you? You were trying to get rid of me! And when that didn't work, you came up with this! And why? Because you're too much of a coward to just stay home and take some pills or jump off a building, so you pull this stunt instead. You're just a big jerk! A big coward! You're like these guys with guns, shooting innocent people! They're just big cowards, and you're no different. They all probably tell themselves they're some sort of hero or notorious or something. They're nothing. You don't even have the guts to live!"

Mitch has gone white.

"Poor Mitch," I say, "you're such a victim, right? Everyone was mean to you. It's all about you, isn't it? You're not just a coward, you're a selfish coward. Well, it's not all about you, you creep! I have a life! I have a family that loves me and I don't want them to lose me. I have friends."

Mitch looks like he could kill me right now. "Shut up!" he screams. "You don't know what it's been like."

"I will know though, won't I? Because if we get out of here alive my life will never be the same. Everyone will know about me. I'll be famous, just like you'll be infamous."

"But in a good way," he objects.

"You don't know that," I say. "They might say it's good police work that finds us, nothing to do with the psychics. Your plan is so full of holes it's ridiculous."

For a few horrible minutes Mitch doesn't say a word. Have I pushed him too far? He tried to hurt me before. Will he try now? Finally he looks up at me and says slowly, as if awakening from a dream, "You're right."

"I know."

"You are! You are. If I'd asked for help—maybe I'd have seen it. I was surrounded by people who would have been happy to help me. Now, now . . . what have I done? It seemed so logical when I was thinking it through. It seemed so right."

"How can killing anyone seem right?" I demand.

He shakes his head. "I don't know. I never talked about it to anyone, just went over and over it in my head until it seemed like it was the only way. And when you turned up, I thought you would ruin it. And then I saw a way to use you."

"That's right," I accuse him. "Use me." I hear a voice again. It's Zaida. "Jade, he's listening. Air, air."

"You need to uncover those air vents," I say to him. "We'll need air if we want to last until they find us."

For a minute I can't tell if he's going to listen to me or revert back to his crazy thinking. But he gets up. He pushes the table over a bit, grabs the piece of wood from the floor, climbs up on the table, and bangs away at the cover. At first it won't give way but he manages to loosen it and then pulls on it with both hands until it falls off.

"Yell for help," I tell him. He does, shouting through the vents.

I watch as he uncovers the other vent as well. And then, somehow, I just know we're going to be all right. We have air. We have water. And I have one of my feelings. Something has changed. We're going to be found.

I tell him that.

"I'm sorry," he says.

"I don't know if that's good enough," I reply.

And then I close my eyes and concentrate. I send our location over and over and over again, while Mitch stands on the table and calls for help.

# SIXTEEN

IT'S NOT LONG AFTER THAT I HEAR SOMETHING. Or maybe it's a voice in my head saying, "They're here."

Whatever it is, I run to the door and start banging and banging and so does Mitch. Finally, we hear a bang in return. And then a muffled voice telling us to hang on, they'll get us out. But it's a long slow process. First, they yell that they have to find a welder, and then once he arrives it takes ages for him to cut through the door. If Mitch hadn't gotten us air we'd be dead. But I know before I'd have let that happen, I would have taken him on.

While we're waiting, Mitch takes three more pills and sits in the corner, sweating, pale and out of it. We don't talk. Finally the door starts to crack and I can hear them shouting "push, push," and the door falls inwards. Police wearing helmets and bulletproof vests barrel in with guns raised. One group sweeps up Mitch, hand-cuffing him and dragging him out, others take me by the arms and lead me into the hallway. Dad is there and he catches me up in a huge hug and won't let go.

Dr. Black is there too, and he just keeps saying over and over how sorry he is. I tell him it isn't his fault.

"Let's get out of here," I say, desperate to see the sun again.

As we walk down the hallway a policeman tells us we need to follow him to the station to make a statement. Dad nods.

"How did you know where we were?" I ask him.

Dr. Black answers. "It was Sonia. She saw you in the basement. Clear as anything, she said."

"So Mitch's experiment worked?" I ask in disbelief.

Dr. Black nods. "It did. But Jade, I need you to know that if I had had any idea at all . . ."

I cut him off. "I'm supposed to be this great psychic, and I didn't have a clue!"

We reach the doors to outside and through the glass see mobs of reporters. Dr. Black tells the police that if we go out the back we should be able to sneak away. We turn around and head to the back exit, where we're hustled into a police cruiser. I sit in the back with Dad, his arm around me. Suddenly I'm so tired I can hardly keep my eyes open.

It feels like we're in the police station in Palm Desert forever. I have to give a statement and sign it and everything. And then they have a child psychologist come in and talk to me. After Dad tells her that Mom is a psychologist and assures her we'll follow up they finally let us go. When we leave we're mobbed by reporters, and I mean mobbed. There must be at least fifty men and women and they swarm us screaming, "Jade! Jade! Over here. What was it like? Can you tell us what it was like? Jade, are you really a psychic? Dr. Joseph, did you think your daughter was going to die in there?" I guess they must have found pictures of us because they seem to recognize us—and then I realize our pictures have probably been all over the news for hours. Mine is certainly easy to get from my web page and Dad's from the university.

The police manage to get us into a car and drive us past the reporters who leap into their own cars and follow us!

Thank goodness Baba's country club is gated and the reporters can't get in. The police let us out in front of our condo and there are Mom and Baba and Marty waiting outside and they all run to us and we're in this group hug for ages. Finally Baba says "You're coming to my house, I have food ready." Of course she does. Wait till I tell her about Zaida!

It's already almost suppertime, and by the time we eat and I manage to tell them the whole story—Marty interrupting every other word with "no way," and "cool" and "you talk to dead people," until Mom has to shush him—it's dark.

Finally Baba says to me, "It was all *B'shert*."

"This was meant to be?" I ask. "You really think so?"

"I believe so," she answers.

Mom shakes her head. She doesn't believe that for a minute. She doesn't believe there's a God directing our every little move. She thinks that kind of God would be a cruel trickster.

Before they can get into a huge fight Dad says we should go back to our condo. Baba gives me a big hug and says she'll be driving us to the airport in the morning. When we get back to the condo Dad has to turn off his cell because it keeps ringing—the media's obviously found his number. But they don't have the number at the rental unit, so Mom is able to talk to Aunt Janeen and to Grandpa and Grandma in Florida. Then the phone rings and she hands it over to me. "Susie," she says.

"Hey," I answer.

"Don't ever do that again!" she scolds me.

"I'll try."

"Can you talk about it? It was all over the news here, you know."

"So I gather."

"And?"

"Can I give you the short version?"

"Know what? Tell me tomorrow when I see you. You sound beat." She pauses. "Heard from Jon?"

"No. And I don't blame him. One thing I realized while all this was happening is that I *was* jealous. The blackness had nothing to do with Cindy! I got it all wrong."

"Don't beat yourself up!" Susie orders me. "It's not science, is it? You see a stupid colour—how are you supposed to figure out what that means? Best guess, really. But hey, this is weird. We've been so panicked about squashing the news of your psychic abilities and now it's all over CNN! I mean, no matter what we did, it got out anyway."

"That's true," I say. And suddenly it hits me. "Oh! That's probably what Baba was thinking when she said it was all meant to be."

There's a beep—call waiting—and I can see the number on the display. "It's Jon!"

"Take it," Susie says. "See you soon."

"Tomorrow," I confirm. I press the flash button.

"Hello," I say.

"Are you all right?"

It's so good to hear Jon's voice.

"I'm not sure."

"What happened?"

"Everyone says I'm a hero. But I'm an idiot," I say.

"What do you mean? Sounds like you handled it really well. Someone at the police station must be leaking your statement because it's on the news about how you talked this maniac into giving up! If that's not a hero, I'm not sure what is."

"I didn't trust you, though, and I trusted him and look where it got me."

"You trusted him?" Jon asks.

I don't want to tell him but he deserves to know. He'll never forgive me anyway, and he might as well hear the truth from me. "I had a bit of a crush on him," I say, not wanting to spare myself. "I was so mad at you for not listening to me about Cindy that I was flattered when Mitch started flirting with me. And now it turns out there's nothing wrong with Cindy and the black-ness was me. Me! It was me being jealous."

For a moment Jon doesn't speak.

"That's what you think?" he says.

"Yes."

"Except it turns out Cindy is a serial cheater. She cheats on all her exams and if I hadn't had your warn-ing I would have been pulled in by her, and helped her plagiarize her essay without realizing it."

"No way!"

"'Fraid so. Those poems I thought were so amazing? e. e. cummings."

Oh, why did I open my mouth? Did I have to blab about my crush on Mitch? Couldn't I have left that out? I don't have a clue what to say next.

"So, you had a crush on this guy?" Jon asks. I can't tell from his voice what he's feeling. Is he furious? Hurt? Disappointed? Or maybe he doesn't care about me enough anymore to be any of those things.

"Well, he seemed to have a crush on me and I guess I was flattered."

"But you managed to get out of it? You got through to him?"

"I got mad," I say. "I got mad and told him the truth."

"Look, Jade...."

I interrupt him. I don't want him to say it. I can't handle it today.

"No, don't say it."

"I have to."

I sigh and wait.

"When I saw you were in trouble, all this seemed silly. I don't blame you. You made a mistake. And I *should* have listened, you were right about that. You didn't need to be jealous, though. I was never interested in her. Never."

147

Tears burn at my eyes. And I know I need to tell him the whole truth.

So I tell him about my fear—the terror that was behind my jealousy all along. "Wouldn't you rather have a normal girlfriend? Someone who's not so weird? And now with this—it won't even be a secret anymore. Everyone at school will know by the time I get home."

"Uh, they all know *now*. My phone is ringing off the hook. I'm famous, too, being your boyfriend. Both newspapers have called me already."

It doesn't escape me that he's still calling himself my boyfriend.

"What have you said?"

"I said that our life is private." He pauses. "And that you're the best girlfriend in the world."

"So, we're okay?" I can hardly believe it. Had it been the other way around and he'd behaved the way I did. . . .

"If it's up to me. What do you say?"

"I say yes."

"Then I say yes too."

For a moment we just sit in silence.

"So, we'll talk tomorrow?" I ask.

"I'll *see* you tomorrow. Take care."

"See you then."

I am frozen in place listening to the dial tone, the phone still at my ear. Slowly I lower it into my lap. And that's when the tears come. When people stick by you even when you don't deserve it, it's pretty amazing. I'm so thankful. But I'm confused too. I was so wrong about everything and yet so right too. I was able to free myself by using my ability. And yet, I got so much "upside down."

Dad and Mom come out to the patio.

"Are you all right?" Mom asks.

"Actually, I'm pretty freaked." I swipe at the tears and Mom leans over to give me a big hug. She sits down beside me and takes my hand. Dad sits down too.

I can see they are both searching for something to say to make me feel better.

Finally Dad says, "Life isn't like a math problem, is it?"

"Neat solutions, you mean?"

"It's kind of messy," says Mom.

"All you can do is your best," says Dad. "I know that sounds trite, and that sometimes our best isn't good enough. But it's all we've got. And you'll learn from this and hopefully you won't make the same mistake, but that doesn't mean you won't make lots of others. We can't live backwards. That would be easy. It's making decisions and not knowing how things will turn out that's hard."

"I never want to be in that head space Mitch was in," I say. "It was horrible."

There's nothing they can say to that. When I think about him, I'm mad and sorry all at once.

"It's going to be crazy when we get home," I say. "Apparently, we're celebrities or something."

"I've had an idea," Mom says. "You're going to have some trouble at school, I know. And I'm going to have some trouble at work, too; likewise Dad at university. Some people will think we're phonies or crazy or delusional. But what if we go on the offence? What if we create a place at home like Dr. Black has made here?"

"What, like an institute to study this?"

Mom nods.

"I might be able to help organize it through the university," Dad says. "The current Dean is pretty open-minded. And maybe Mom could be team leader."

"And leave your practice?"

"From what Dad tells me, Dr. Black started doing this because he needed answers. Well, he's not the only one. And it's better to do something positive than to try to pretend none of this is happening. Baba said that maybe you should just own up. Now you have to. And we'd like to be behind you, or with you, or however you want to see it."

Tears come to my eyes again. Whatever it all means, I know I'm not alone. My friends, my boyfriend, my family—hey, even my dead family like Zaida—are all with me. That makes it okay.

I am all right.